A Lady's Christmas

The Everton Domestic Society

A.S. Fenichel

A LADY'S PAST by A.S. Fenichel

Copyright © 2023 by A.S. Fenichel

Edited by Oopsie Daisy Edits

Cover design by Dar Albert at Wicked Smart Designs

A Lady's Christmas

The only bad part about growing up as the ward of the Duke of Stratham was the occasional visits from his nephew and heir, Theo. Unable to remember her parents, Stratham was the only father Gwen ever had, and now he's gone too. Rather than suffer the indignity of living under the rule of her nemesis, she joined The Everton Domestic Society. At least she can be of use to someone. She's fully capable of running a large estate and is of the age to make her own decisions.

Upon arrival at his newly inherited estate, Theo Dandridge, the sixth Duke of Stratham, finds the grounds and house in perfect order. The only thing amiss is his uncle's ward, who is nowhere to be found. Gwen has always been a burr under his saddle and now he's forced to go fetch her from her new employer. Most say that she is kind—to everyone but him—and that children love her. According to the staff, she's been running the ducal estates for six years. After spending so many years focused on Gwen's flaws, perhaps it's Theo's character that needs investigation...

Chapter One

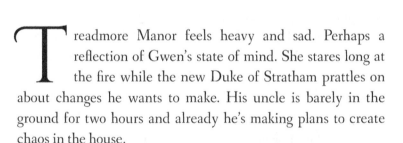

Treadmore Manor feels heavy and sad. Perhaps a reflection of Gwen's state of mind. She stares long at the fire while the new Duke of Stratham prattles on about changes he wants to make. His uncle is barely in the ground for two hours and already he's making plans to create chaos in the house.

To Theo Dandridge, it's just an asset, but to Gwen, it is the only home she's ever known. At least the only one she can remember.

"Are you listening to me, Gwendolyn?" Theo's voice clips the air, taking away the warmth of the fire.

Gazing toward the desk, Gwen sighs. "I hear you, Your Grace."

It must be her imagination, but she'd have sworn he cringed at his new title. No. It must be a trick of the light. He has no feelings and therefore can't possibly care about the fact that his only living relative is no more.

He taps some papers into a stack and places them in the bin

to be dealt with later. Crossing the room, he sits next to Gwen on the settee. For a full minute, he toys with a tiny thread that has come loose on the blue damask cushion. "I have to go abroad for the next month. I'll be in France and then Italy. Should you need to reach me, I've given Mrs. Tubbs my address."

"I can't imagine that would be necessary, Your Grace." Gwen glances at him, wishing he wasn't so damned good-looking. His blue eyes surrounded by dark lashes are hard to look away from, but she forces her gaze back to the fire.

Letting out a long breath, he touches her arm. "Gwendolyn, you have called me Theo all of our lives, I see no reason for the formal address now."

Sadly, this is possibly the nicest thing he's ever said to her. "Just remembering my place. You are the duke now." She stares at his hand on her arm. Warmth spreads from his touch.

He jerks away as if burned. "You didn't call my uncle by his title."

"He was the only father I ever knew. I called him papa because when I came here, I didn't know any better. The late duke was kind and allowed the endearment even after I was old enough to be told the truth. You are certainly not my father or my brother." Wishing she could hit him so hard that he would feel a fraction of her pain at losing Alden Dandridge wouldn't make Theo wise, though it might make her feel better. Still, she refrained.

Theo's expression softens and he leans toward her. Raising his hand, he brushes a wayward strand of hair away from her cheek.

Years of childhood bickering and boyish antics from him make her jerk away from his touch.

Rather than pull back, he leans in closer. "No. I am not your relation by blood."

Breath stuck in her throat, she's mesmerized by his stare and his handsome face when he's not scowling. "No."

As if just realizing his dislike of her, he shakes his head and sits up straight. Clearing his throat, he stands. With his hands behind his back, he paces the study. "I have things to attend to abroad and no one to send in my stead. I'm sure you'll manage to keep busy here as you always have. When I return, we'll need to hire you a chaperone for propriety. My uncle may have been fatherly, but I certainly am not."

The idea of living under Theo's rule puts a knot in her stomach. Returning her gaze to the fire, she nods. It's taking a great deal of energy to keep from crying in front of him. Rather than engaging in a lengthy discussion about what she does as the acting steward of this estate and the lady of the house is pointless. He'd never believe her anyway. "Have a safe trip, Your Grace."

He harrumphs. "You know, Gwendolyn, he was my uncle. I have suffered a loss as well."

Shaking, she stands and faces him. "You happen by Tread-more Manor on occasion at Christmas and Easter as if you're doing someone a favor by showing up. Then you act as if being here is a great inconvenience. You write once a month to see that your allowance is deposited. When you are here, you plague me with errands and other chores you believe should be my responsibility to handle while having no idea of what I actually do from day to day. You're rude and demanding. Since your uncle's death, I've detected no sign that you mourn him in the slightest. All you have done is attend a funeral that I arranged and tell me of your plans to change the only home I have ever known."

Gathering her wits, she lowers her voice. "You have every right to change what you want in this estate, but do not expect *me* to change to suit you." Drawing a long breath and dashing away a tear, she adds, "I'm sorry for your loss, Your Grace."

Theo opens his mouth and closes it again. He looks from one end of the room to the other, then back at her. Without voicing whatever thoughts caused his eyes to flash with anger, he turns and storms out of the library.

Two Weeks Later

Gwen Carter makes every effort to not fidget in the chair as she waits for Jane Everton to read through her application to become an Everton Lady. She glances at the books lining two walls, including the one behind Lady Jane. At the base of the shelves, flanking the desk, are two benches with moss-green cushions. It looks like a perfect place to read.

A large window faces the street at Gwen's back, but she listens to the people, horses, and carts making their way through the day while her future hangs in the balance.

Lady Jane's expression is calm as she turns the page, then her dark brows rise, and she smooths her hand over her hair, which is pulled back in a severe bun. "You have been running the estates of the Duke of Stratham for the past six years?"

"Yes, my lady." Gwen's voice cracks and she clears her throat.

Jane gazes at Gwen. "Do not think me indelicate, Miss Carter, but how old are you?"

Pulling her shoulders back, Gwen lifts her chin. "I'm three and twenty."

"I see. You must have shown a gift for numbers for the fifth duke to have trusted you with such a task." Jane draws a deep breath and stands. Tall and slender, there is nothing delicate about Lady Jane Everton. Her brown eyes are kind and her jaw is strong. As she looks out the front window, there's the slightest rise of her eyebrows, but she gives away none of what's going on in her mind.

Gwen's heart sinks. She's being put out and will have no choice but to go back to Treadmore and be lorded over by Theo and whoever he hires to chaperone her. Standing, she bites her lip to keep any emotions from showing.

After pulling the cord near the hearth, Jane takes a book from her desk drawer and holds it out toward Gwen. "This is *The Everton Lady's Companion*. I suggest you study our rules and ideals."

The door opens and a servant enters. She's a large woman with graying brown hair, light-blue eyes, and a kind expression. "My lady?"

"Ah, Mrs. Grimsby. Will you make up a room for Miss Carter? She'll be starting as an Everton Lady, and I imagine she's in need of some rest before dinner. Will you inform Lady Chervil that we have a new Everton Lady who will require a chaperone in the near future?" Lady Jane folds her hands in front of her waist. "Has Lord Rupert returned from court yet?"

Mrs. Grimsby smiles. "I'll have the blue room ready in a blink. It has a lovely view of the garden. His lordship arrived five minutes ago and has gone up to change."

"Thank you." Jane's cheeks turn slightly pink, which seems out of place, but lovely at the same time.

Not sure what to do, Gwen stares for several moments at the book in her hand. "You're accepting me?"

"Of course," Jane says with a hint of a smile. "You're

perfectly suited to the work. I have several clients who will benefit from your assistance with their accounts and general household organization." She brushes out her skirt and checks her reflection in the glass over the fireplace. There's a serenity about Lady Jane Everton that is admirable.

"Thank you." Gwen turns to follow the housekeeper out of the office.

"Miss Carter?" Jane asks. "May I ask why the former duke didn't bring you out and find you a husband?"

Heart pounding, Gwen should be used to this question, but she never has liked talking about it. "I think he considered me a child even after I'd grown, and in the last few years, his mind wasn't what it aught be."

Frowning, Jane says, "Perhaps he needed a woman's advice on the subject." She shakes off whatever she'd been thinking, and her expression returns to serenity. "You are still young and if you wished to marry, I believe there are many suitable men who would court you."

"I'm not interested in being courted." It comes out too harsh. Gwen adds, "I don't think I'm suited for marriage, my lady."

"Many ladies say that until they meet the man who they can love." If she was going to say more, the door opening stopped her.

A tall man with dark hair and a thin beard that runs along his jaw and merges with a well-waxed mustache enters. His blue eyes survey the room before he grins and bows. "Good afternoon."

Jane smiles and her eyes light up. "Miss Carter, this is my husband, Lord Rupert."

Amazed at the obvious affection the two convey in just a brief glance at each other, Gwen is slightly embarrassed. She curtsies. "How do you do, my lord?"

"Miss Carter. Will you be joining our home?" Rupert asks as he shakes her hand.

"Yes, sir."

"Splendid." His grin is contagious.

Jane says, "Mrs. Grimsby was just about to show Miss Carter to her room so that she can have a rest before dinner."

"Of course. Don't let me keep you." He moves aside so that Gwen can pass and follow the housekeeper out.

In the foyer, Mrs. Grimsby takes Gwen's arm and leads her up the tall staircase. "You'll do just fine here, miss. If you're kind and you work hard, the Evertons will take good care of you."

"That sounds easy enough." Gwen clutches *The Everton Companion* to her side as they step into a bedroom with wooden wainscoting and blue wallpaper composed of vertical lines in a slightly darker shade. "I thought they would turn me away." She turns to give the room her full attention.

The bed is larger than the one she had at home and the pale-blue bedding has a hint of lace at the edges. Dark-blue curtains hang at four posts and match those pulled back at the large window. The fireplace is dark, but an overstuffed chair is placed in a cozy spot nearby. At the window stands a lady's desk and chair with a light-blue bud vase on the corner. "This is lovely."

"I'm pleased you think so." Mrs. Grimsby examines the room. "I'll have one of the girls come up and make you a nice fire and we'll get you some paper, pen, and ink in case you have need. Is there anything else I can do for you, Miss Carter?"

"You are too kind. I think I'll be fine. What time is dinner?" Gwen takes off her pelisse and looks out the window, which faces a garden. It's grown colder and the flowers are no longer in bloom, but several trees have red and golden leaves. It's lovely.

"Dinner is at seven and the Evertons are very keen on promptness."

"I'll be on time." As soon as she's alone, Gwen flops on the bed. "I did it."

Her next thought is, *what have I done?*

Chapter Two

"What do you mean, she's not here?" Theo's heart lodges in his throat. He knows he shouldn't yell at the staff, but Mrs. Tubbs just told him that Gwen left Treadmore three weeks ago.

"Your Grace, as I said, Miss Carter has left. You will find a letter on your desk with the rest of the accounts she left for whomever you hire as your new steward." Mrs. Tubbs cocks her head as if ready for his acceptance of the situation.

How can he possibly accept that his ward had left? "What do you mean, new steward? Where is Dockerty?"

Eyes wide, Mrs. Tubbs folds her arms under her large bosom and takes a step back toward the doorway. "Mr. Dockerty passed away six years ago, Your Grace. I thought your uncle would have told you."

Searching his memory, Theo can find no recollection, though he had been sowing oats and so forth for a good portion of the six years prior. "He might have done, but clearly, I've forgotten. Who has been the steward since then and why would they not continue their job?"

"Why, Miss Gwen took care of all the accounts as well as all the household duties. She left you a listing of all accounts before she left." Mrs. Tubbs gapes at him as if it's impossible he didn't know. She has been the housekeeper at Treadmore for longer than Theo has been alive. She's a nice woman who keeps a clean, orderly home.

Theo is tempted to do her harm for the first time in his life. "Why isn't Gwendolyn here?"

The butler, George Noble, pushes past Mrs. Tubbs. Perhaps he senses the duke's growing anger. "She decided to leave of her own accord, Your Grace. Perhaps you might read her correspondence."

Theo closes his eyes and takes a deep breath to keep his temper in check. Even in her absence, Gwendolyn Carter knows just how to drive him to rage. "You may both go. I will read the letter."

Before the words are fully out of his mouth, both the butler and the housekeeper flee the library and the door shuts.

On the corner of his uncle's desk is a very neat stack of documents and at the very top, an envelope. *Theodore Dandridge, Duke of Stratham* is written in Gwen's graceful handwriting. Sitting, he uses the old knife with the initials *ADD* etched on the handle to open the envelope. Rubbing his thumb over the engraving, he sighs. "She never gave *you* all this trouble, Uncle. Why does she vex me? I should just let her go and say good riddance."

He opens the letter. The knot that formed in his chest the moment he'd learned that Gwen had left grows tighter.

Your Grace,

Since I was entrusted to your departed uncle by my parents at the time of their deaths, I feel I'm only a burden to you. I now relieve you of that responsibility. My parents and the late duke were the best of friends, and so I'm sure at the time, it made sense to leave their small child in Alden Dandridge's caring hands.

My love for your uncle kept me at Treadmore past the time when I should have either married or found employment. I'm no longer a child, and it's far past the time for me to find my own way in the world. I'm in no danger as I've made arrangements for suitable employment.

You will find an account of all household and estate details at the top of the documents. Your new steward should have no problems handling things going forward, as all have been kept in order since the time of Mr. Dockerty's passing.

I hope you will be well and remember to take care of yourself. I know you don't like vegetables, but they are good for your health and you should try to eat several servings a day. Your affection for the horses is a good way to stay fit, you might also take up walking and perhaps other outdoor activities.

In no time, you will find a wife to take over the household duties. Until then, Mrs. Tubbs will assist you.

Wishing you all the best,
Gwendolyn E. Carter

Sitting with the letter in his hand for a long time, it's at once infuriating that she's left him and amusing that she felt the need to remind him to eat his vegetables.

Certain that the staff knows where she's gone and equally sure they are sworn to secrecy, he will need to find a way to wheedle the information out of them.

After reading the letter a second time, he studies the immaculately kept accounts that detail the solid ground the estates are on. Farms are paying nicely and regularly. At the bottom of the yearly account in the expenses column is listed "Christmas Ball" but a black mark has been scratched through.

At the far side of the account, she has written "canceled" in the same neat handwriting.

He rings for the butler.

A moment later, Noble steps inside the library. "Your Grace?"

"Why has the Christmas Ball at Crestworth House been cancelled?" He hasn't attended one in years, but if memory serves, it's very popular, and all the local people and tenants are invited.

Noble clears his throat. "I suppose with the former duke having passed, Miss Carter thought the tradition would fall by the wayside."

Of course, she thinks he'd have no interest in parties that lack an upper-crust attendance and a monetary goal. He has no one to blame but himself. His behavior has never been filled with warmth or sentiment. So why now does he want his uncle's ward back at Treadmore?

Every time he looks at the hearth, the image of Gwen's tear-stained cheek on the day of the funeral haunts him. He saw she was holding in her emotions and wanted to comfort her. It's too late for that. He'd spent more than half his life avoiding or berating her. She'd have rejected any kindness from him, and who could blame her?

"I assume that Gwendolyn made all of those arrangements as well." He points to the stack of accounting to his left.

Breaking eye contact, Noble shifts on his feet. "Um, well, in the last few years, your uncle was not himself and many details began to be unattended. Miss Carter is a very capable young woman, and she cared for your uncle very much. Rather than let the estate suffer, she began to handle the daily work of the steward and the master."

Narrowing his gaze, the mention of eating his vegetables returns to the forefront of Theo's mind. "Did she also handle all the work that might be destined for the lady of the house if there had ever been one?"

Noble seems to realize he's fidgeting and stands up straight with his hands at his back. "She did, Your Grace."

"Good lord, when did she find time to sleep?" Theo stares at the mountain of paper stating every account, holding, and other financial minutia and then looks back at the hearth. "Where did she go, Noble?"

"She asked us not to say, sir." There must be something a bit desperate in Theo's eyes, because Noble sighs when the duke looks up at him. "To The Everton Domestic Society. She wrote two weeks ago that she'd gained employment and is quite comfortable."

"Thank you. You may go."

Alone, Theo had nothing but regret to ponder.

He had never met anyone in all his travels who riled him the way Gwen could. He also never met anyone he was as happy to see after a long journey. Perhaps he should have been nicer, but when he was young, she had his uncle's attention, and he knew what everyone expected of him. Once he was older, he'd enjoyed seeing her in fits of anger and nothing gave him more pleasure than when they would spar with words.

It bore a resemblance to becoming the duke. He'd known for a long time that he would be Duke of Stratham one day. His father was dead, and his uncle had no children. He knew the title would fall to him, but he'd never considered that it would actually happen. When his uncle's mind began to show signs of wandering, he'd written it off as the vagaries of aging. Four years earlier at Easter, he'd won a chess match with his uncle for the first time. At the time, he'd been thrilled, but now he knew it was a sad day. He should have spent more time at Treadmore.

The Everton Domestic Society is housed in a nice part of town. The house is well-appointed and cheerful. An ancient butler let Theo in and showed him into a parlor at the front of the house. The furniture is very fine with varying shades of gold and brown. Fresh flowers sit on the coffee table and on top of the grand piano stationed in the front window.

Theo turns when the door opens.

A crease forms between Gwen's eyes. "Your Grace, what are you doing here?" The red in her hair catches the sunlight streaming through the room, and her green eyes flash with emotions.

Daring not to ask if her question is meant kindly or accusatory, he bows. "I returned home and found you gone. I came to see you and bring you back to Treadmore."

"I'm not going back." Her mouth opens to say more, but a maid enters.

"Shall I bring some tea, Miss Carter?"

It looks as if Gwen is biting the inside of her cheek, probably to keep herself from saying something cutting. She sighs. "Your Grace, would you care for some tea?"

Theo moves to the front of a chair placed near the coffee table. "If you will join me, Gwendolyn, I would be delighted."

She whispers something he can't make out. "Tea, please, May."

May bobs and rushes out the door.

The caution in Gwen's expression is his fault, so he stays calm, despite his wish to demand she sit and then pack and come home. "Please, sit, Gwendolyn."

"Miss Carter would be more appropriate." Her voice is

formal as she crosses to the settee and sits. "I'm not going to leave Everton."

"You don't need employment. You are my responsibility." It's not easy to keep his voice from rising, but before he came, he swore he wouldn't get angry with her.

"I am not anyone's responsibility. I was the ward of your uncle, not his title. You didn't inherit me with the estates and fortune, Your Grace." The strain in her voice pushes his temper to the surface.

Biting his tongue does little to help when she's accusing him of treating her like a possession. "I did inherit all the responsibilities of the Duke of Stratham and you are among them. There is no reason for you to take employment like a common woman with no other means. You're the daughter of a gentleman, Gwendolyn."

Standing in the open door, a tall woman with dark hair pulled back from her face clears her throat. Her cheekbones are very high and her expression is serene. "Many of the Everton Ladies are the daughters of gentlemen, Your Grace."

Theo and Gwen stand as she enters. Gwen says, "Lady Jane Everton, may I introduce the Duke of Stratham."

Bowing, Theo wishes he'd had more time alone with Gwen. The rise of voices was probably what brought the lady of the house to the parlor, so he has no one to blame but himself, once again. "My lady, it's a pleasure to meet you."

Jane sits. "The pleasure is mine."

May brings the tea tray and places it on the table.

Jane pours while silence fills the room. Once she's handed each of them a cup, she says, "I couldn't help overhearing that you wish for Miss Carter to return to your estate."

"Yes, my lady. She belongs at Treadmore. I fail to understand what drove her to seek another life." Theo places the cup and saucer on the table without drinking a single drop.

Chapter Three

G wen thought Theo would be happy to have her out from underfoot. She never dreamed he'd bother to come and find her. Well, maybe she thought he might be curious and that's why she asked the staff to keep her whereabouts from him. She sips her tea and works up a fine rage, but holds her tongue because Lady Jane is present.

"Miss Carter, I gather from your loud reaction that you don't wish to return with the duke?" Jane's expression never wavers from calm assurance.

"I have no intention of leaving The Everton Domestic Society. Now that I have a few clients who need my help, I have purpose." Gwen puts her cup down and picks a biscuit from the tray.

"What kind of work are you doing?" Theo takes a biscuit as well and eats it in one bite.

Nibbling on a corner, she frowns. He has some nerve to come here asking questions about her life. He didn't come home but once or twice a year, even after his uncle became ill.

"I'm helping the Earl of Baskin with his accounts, and a widow with some financial issues. I'm doing just fine here."

Fire flashes in his eyes. "I assume you have a chaperone when visiting Lord Baskin."

Jane speaks before Gwen can formulate a good snipe back at him. "All Everton Ladies are accompanied by a suitable chaperone when the situation warrants. Mrs. Chervil accompanies Miss Carter to her appointments and if a client needs her to stay at their estate, Mrs. Chervil will go along to keep everything very proper."

"Stay at Baskin's estate. No. I forbid it. Phillip Baskin is a rake. He is not suitable company for a young lady."

Jumping up, Gwen says, "You can't forbid anything. I'm not your sister and I'm not your ward. I'm nothing to you. Just because your uncle was like a father to me does not make you my keeper." She dashes away the aggravating tears that force their way out.

Theo stands, but he doesn't raise his voice. He stares at his feet for a moment before his calm tone cuts the silence. "I am not your keeper or your brother, Gwen. I have behaved badly over the years, and I can offer no good explanation for that." He looks her in the eyes. "However, I'd like to think having grown up together, we are a bit more than nothing to each other." He closes his eyes, and when he opens them, the blue irises seem brighter than before. "I haven't found anyone to take on the job of steward. I need you to come home. The estate in Derbyshire has had several livestock issues, which I can't explain. I have to go there this week and need you to come with me. I tried taking care of the situation via correspondence, but Mr. Green didn't respond."

"Mr. Green is an excellent farmer, but he can't read." Her stomach flutters at the soft tones of Theo's voice and his use of the name she prefers. "You need to speak to him and find out what happened." The idea that there may have been a blight on the Derbyshire farms increases Gwen's anxiety. Those poor people can't afford to lose the farms.

Leaning back to gaze up at the two of them standing around the table, Jane says, "I have a thought."

They both turn toward her. Gwen wishes she could run up to her room and cry until the feeling of loneliness goes away. Why does Theo's presence and inevitable departure make her feel so alone?

Jane waits for them to sit, and she returns to her upright posture. "Perhaps Miss Carter can remain an Everton Lady and she can still assist you, Your Grace. You could hire her to go to Derbyshire and sort out your farming issues. Perhaps she'd be willing to stay on and handle the estates. She's quite capable of finding you a permanent steward to replace her for the long term."

Theo blinks several times. "I would pay her to do what she's been doing for the past six years."

"I did that for your uncle, not money." The idea of going home isn't terrible. Still, all Theo ever does is find fault in her.

Seeming to ignore her statement, he says, "I also need help with the Christmas Ball."

Shock rockets through her. Why would he hold the ball? "You're having the ball?"

"It's tradition. One you started, if memory serves." His voice has that tone that sends shivers through her belly once again.

"You never cared about the ball in the past." She must stand her ground. Just because he can say and do decent things from time to time doesn't make him a nice person. Almost twenty years of knowing him has shown he can be impossible and demanding.

"I care. In the past, my focus was elsewhere, I'll admit."

Is that regret in his voice?

No. Impossible. He's too arrogant to regret anything.

If she says no, she'll look spiteful in front of Lady Jane. *The Everton Companion* says she has to be kind and thoughtful at all times, even if Theo Dandridge deserves none of it. "If his grace agrees to my taking control of things, finding a replacement, and allowing Mrs. Chervil to accompany me, I'll agree to the contract."

"Will Miss Carter agree to teach me how she keeps the books and help with the preparations for the Christmas Ball?" A smile lights his eyes even though his expression stays serious and businesslike.

"I agree." Her heart pounds so hard it's a small miracle that she got the words out. "Having a duke on my resume will bode well for my future at Everton."

The joy fades from his gaze.

Jane claps her hands. "That's settled then. I'll draw up a contract. I do have one question, Your Grace."

"Of course." Theo turns all his attention to Lady Jane.

Gwen wants to pinch herself for wanting him to look at her again.

"Why didn't your uncle bring Miss Carter out into society for a season or two? I'm sure she might have made a very fine match if she'd had the opportunity." Jane sips the last of her tea and places it on the tray.

Neck red, Theo's chest rises and falls. "I'm not sure what the answer to that is, my lady. He must have had his reasons, or perhaps his view of Miss Carter was that of a little girl, and he never considered that she would want another life."

"Hmm. Perhaps. I assume you are aware that Miss Carter is a grown woman, and you will remain a gentleman at all times?" Jane's voice is full of warning.

"Of course," he says then looks at Gwen with the fire back in those beautiful blue eyes.

The estate in Derbyshire is large, with twenty bedrooms, two ballrooms, an extensive library, a dining room, and four parlors. Theo traveled there ahead of the ladies to make sure all was in order. It shouldn't matter, since if anything is amiss, Gwen will set it to rights, but oddly, he wants to impress her.

Ridiculous, he admonishes himself. She needs to know that she can stay if she wants, and if that means affording her a small salary, that's what he'll do. He promised his uncle he'd always look after her. However, the current situation was not what Alden Dandridge had in mind.

In yellow livery, the footmen rushed around him, clearing away furniture coverings while maids cleaned floors and started fires in hearths. It's a very organized kind of chaos that has very little need of Noble's attention. Still, the man watches as he passes through each room, verifying that everything is done perfectly.

"Your grace, you needn't worry." The housekeep stops her own pass through the front parlor. "I'll see that the house is ready."

"They shall be here in a few hours. I don't wish them to find the place rolling in dust and chilled without fires in the hearths." Whatever has gotten into him, it's completely new and not at all dignified.

Mrs. Hampton has been the housekeeper at Crestworth House since he was a boy. She gave him sweets when he was punished and cooled his fever when he was ill. Patient as ever, she sighs. "Lamb has the footmen all in order. You have no valet, so one of them will help you while you're here, though you're a duke now and really should hire someone permanently. I have the other staff working as you can see. It will all be done before the ladies arrive from London. You have my word. Cook has a fine supper in the works with some of Miss Carter's favorites."

He relaxes his stiff shoulders and sighs. "Of course, you will make this all fine, just as you always have, Mrs. Hampton. Forgive me. I can't imagine why I'm worried. It's not as if Miss Carter is a stranger."

"Certainly not." The years have added a few pounds to Mrs. Hampton and a few wrinkles as well, but her eyes are the same sharp brown as they ever were. Taking his arm, she leads him toward the back garden. "Do you remember when little Gwen first came to live with your uncle?"

"I was ten." He pats her hand, remembering all the times she was kind to him.

"Yes, and a fine strapping boy you were. Gwen was just five years old and had lost her parents. She was terrified, but you took her hand and showed her the lovely bedroom your uncle had redecorated for her. I imagine the weeks it took to sort out the legal guardianship had been the worst for our little Gwen. Stuck in an orphanage with no idea of why all of that sorrow had been heaped on her."

"She was so small. She's not much bigger now." He laughs, as does Mrs. Hampton.

When they reach the center of the garden with its tall trees and surrounding hedges, they sit and Mrs. Hampton says, "She's petite, but a fine young lady. I wonder why his grace never found her a husband?"

"You're the second person to ask me that this week."

Raising her eyebrows, Mrs. Hampton stands. "Perhaps you should give the answer some thought. In the meantime, stay out of the house for an hour and let us get our work done."

Having been handled, he chuckles and does as he's told. Why hadn't Uncle found Gwen a husband? She's certainly pretty enough and more than bright enough to have attracted a great many men of good standing. In fact, she's more beautiful every time he sees her. She manages the house in London, this estate, and the smaller holdings as well, and she'd been doing it since she was a girl.

"I should have come home more and helped her," he says to the empty garden. Regret wouldn't do any good now. He'd find a way to make it right. She's only three and twenty, he could still find her a husband if that's what she wants. Don't all women want to get married and have children?

His stomach burns with the idea of all the stupid sods who will try to woo her. Fortune hunters will come out of the woodwork when they find out he'll give her a nice dowry.

Why was it so important to her to leave him and the life she knew?

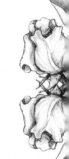

Chapter Four

Crestworth House sits on a fine piece of property with a reflecting pool to show off the beautiful place. "Look, Mrs. Chervil. It's a fine place, is it not?"

Blinking awake, Mrs. Honoria Chervil sits up and leans toward the carriage window. "Oh my. It's a fine house indeed. Did you spend much time here as a child?"

Nodding, Gwen smiles. "This is where I first met my adopted father and the new duke too. It was daunting to drive up with the mail, only then to be dropped off at the front door. I thought I'd be locked in one of those towers like in the storybooks."

Lady Chervil's kind eyes became glassy with unshed tears and her sunny smile faltered. "How terrible for you, my dear. All alone in the world and having to face a new life all by yourself."

Shrugging, Gwen banishes the memories to the back of her mind. "Perhaps it gave me the strength to leave my life and join

The Everton Domestic Society. If a small girl could survive, I can manage now."

"I'm sure you will flourish, Gwen." Leaning back, Lady Chervil watches the park-like gardens roll past on the long drive.

"I'll admit, I'm a bit nervous. Theo Dandridge can be difficult. I'd be mortified if he were rude to you." Gwen forces herself to stop fussing with the front of her dress.

"Lady Jane said he was a perfect gentleman when he came to call." With a raise of her brows, Lady Chervil waits for more information.

It wouldn't do to lie about the meeting. "We argued loud enough for Lady Jane to come in. It was as much my fault as his, but it's obvious we can't get along."

"It's big of you to take some of the blame. Don't fret about me. I've yet to meet a duke I couldn't handle." Amusement sparkles in Lady Chervil's eyes as if ready for the challenge.

The carriage pulls to a stop at the front and Gwen draws a deep breath as a footman in yellow livery opens the door.

Lady Chervil takes the young man's arm and steps out. "Oh, Your Grace, what a lovely place you have. Gwen has told me so much about you, I feel we are old friends."

"Indeed, madam. You have me at a disadvantage." Theo's full, deep voice reaches Gwen.

Another breath and Gwen takes the footman's arm. "Thank you, Andrew."

Andrew almost smiles and nods to hide the slip. "Miss Carter."

Gwen steps forward and grins at all the staff and how sharp they look, waiting on the steps to greet her. With a brief curtsy, she avoids Theo's gaze. "Your Grace. May I introduce Lady Honoria Chervil."

He takes Honoria's hand and bows over it. "A pleasure to meet you, my lady."

"The pleasure is mine, Your Grace." Honoria bats her eyelashes.

It's not easy, but Gwen holds in her amusement. "It was nice of you to assemble the staff. I haven't seen them in some time. Your uncle had not been well enough to travel north in a few years."

His silence forces her to look him in the eyes. They are the same clear blue but somehow look kinder than they have in the past and they smile at her. "There you are. I would like to take credit, but the staff insisted on greeting you properly. It seems they have missed you very much."

Knowing he could have ordered them to stay at their posts, a tingle of warmth washes over her. "I'll just say hello and then we can get to work."

Offering Lady Chervil his arm, he says, "Take your time, Gwendolyn. I've arranged for tea to be served in the grand parlor when we're ready and then I'm sure you and Lady Chervil will wish to rest after your journey. We can go and see Mr. Green in the morning if you're feeling up to it."

One by one, Gwen meets with each member of the Crestworth House staff. The scullery maid was just a girl the last time Gwen saw her and now she's full grown and says she's sixteen. So much time has passed and she feels like she's missed too much.

Lamb gives her a curt bow but a warm smile.

Mrs. Hampton pulls her into a warm hug. "I know I shouldn't hug you now that you're a fine lady, Miss Carter, but oh, how we've missed you."

"I've missed you too." It's so nice to be held and cared for. It's been so long since she's had anyone to hug her. Gwen has to dash away a tear before anyone can see.

The way Theo looks at her, she worries he may have seen the weakness. Since he doesn't tease her about it, he must not have seen it. He never misses an opportunity to point out her flaws.

In the parlor, he waits until she and Lady Chervil sit before he does. "I'm very pleased you're here."

"Because you're getting what you want?" Of course, he's happy. He thinks he's won something. It's best to get the truth out all at once. "I'm in the employ of The Everton Domestic Society, Your Grace. I'm here to do a job and once it's complete, I will leave here and you shall not control my life."

Lady Chervil's eyes widen. "I hope tea will arrive soon."

Theo's forehead crinkles, and he stares at his shoes for a long moment before meeting Gwen's gaze. "I know your opinion of me is poor and that it is not unfairly so. I have not been kind to you over the years. Allow me to say that I am not proud of my behavior and perhaps after a time, we can discuss it as friends."

"On the one hand, I think you're apologizing, but on the other, I think you're setting up some elaborate plan. As such, I'm left in disbelief." Gwen should thank him and let it go, but except for some random moments when he was kind, he had been the worst part of her life.

"I'm sorry, Gwendolyn. I will endeavor to earn your friendship." The sincerity in his voice and expression takes her by surprise and a knot forms in her chest.

"Well, that's a lovely start," Lady Chervil chirps.

Tricia, the maid, brings the tea, saving Gwen from responding.

In her bedroom, Gwen paces and tries to figure out what it is that Theo is really after.

"You'll wear a path in that rug if you keep going like that." Lady Chervil breezes in wearing a flowing lavender dress. "Are you going to change for dinner?"

Stepping behind the dressing screen, Gwen begins to change. "I didn't realize so much time had passed."

"What has you so upset?"

Gwen wants to interview all the servants rather than dine with Theo, who is acting so strange. "I just don't understand why the duke is so, so..."

"Handsome, gracious, warm, or was charming the word you were looking for, my dear?"

"I need someone to button this dress." Crossing the room, Gwen pulls the cord for a maid before sitting on the edge of the bed.

Honoria, sitting on the chair at the small writing desk, fusses with a bit of lace at the waist of her bodice. "You really should travel with a maid."

"I didn't bring my maid when I left home to join the society. I found her a good position in the home of the Earl of Brent." Unexpected emotions rise inside Gwen, and she has to take several deep breaths to push them down.

There's a knock at the door before it opens and Ella the upstairs maid pokes her head in. "Did you need something, miss?"

"Yes, Ella. Can you help me dress?"

With a bright smile, Ella comes and closes the door.

Gwen stands so her dress can button up the back. "Thank you." Returning to the conversation with Honoria, Gwen says, "He has never been nice to me. I know you see a handsome charming duke, but I see a boy who tormented me and a man who ignored his uncle most of the time, and when he did grace us with his presence, he criticized everything. I was the most flawed of all his complaints."

"Perhaps he's seen the error of his ways." Honoria smiles and fusses with her emerald ring.

"He's up to something. I just have to figure out what it is."

"There you are, miss." Ella brushes out the skirt.

"You look lovely, Gwen." Honoria's bright happy company is welcome.

"Thank you both."

Once Ella leaves, Honoria says, "He may have realized he missed you when he came home and found you gone."

For a brief second, Gwen considers this. "No. He may miss all the things I did to keep his estates running and profitable, but he certainly never missed me."

"I noticed when we drove up and you mentioned having first met the duke here, you smiled. So, it wasn't always contentious between the two of you." Honoria may seem like she's frivolous and not paying attention, but clearly, she's keenly observant.

Gwen wishes she could say that Theo had always been one thing or the other, but there have been times when he was kind and perhaps it's those glimpses of the man he could be that make her so critical of his behavior in general. "He was very kind to a small child when she was afraid and brokenhearted. On that day, I thought it might all be all right, if this boy could be my friend. We had two lovely weeks playing in the gardens while I got to know my new home and the duke."

"It sounds lovely." Honoria smiles. "What changed?"

A knot forms in Gwen's chest. "He had to go back to school and then we didn't see him for several years. When he returned, he was twelve and full of himself. I don't know why he teased and tormented me, but after that, he was horrible every summer until he went to Oxford. Then he came less often."

"Was he never again the kind boy you met that first summer?" The sympathy in Honoria's eyes makes Gwen want to cry.

"From time to time, he would forget himself and be kind. When I was sixteen, I had a cat who had a litter of kittens and all were stillborn. I was devastated and cried for many long hours. Theo came to the barn and held me while I cried. He took the little babies away and dug a grave. He was warmer on that day than when we buried the duke."

"He may have had his reasons for his treatment of you, Gwen. I don't condone it, but the man I just met was charming and courteous. He looked at you with affection and you barely gazed at him. He did offer an apology. Perhaps you should try to get along with him at least while you're working for him." Honoria stands. "I'm going down for a glass of wine before dinner. Will you join me?"

Should she forgive him and forget all the times when they might have been friends? Should she also forget that it took him months to come after she wrote to him that his uncle was gravely ill? It would be the right thing to do, but she didn't know if she was a good enough person to let all of that go. "Of course."

Chapter Five

Mr. Green softens his expression the moment he sees Gwen. In fact, she gets the stoic farmer telling a long story about some wild dogs that have been terrorizing the area. No one knows where the dogs came from, but for the last six months, they've killed over forty chickens and fifteen piglets in the neighborhood.

Horrified that he'd known nothing about the problem and ashamed that he'd stayed away from his responsibilities, Theo listens to everything Mr. Green has to say.

With a brief look at Gwen, as focuses on Mr. Green, Theo gives the farmer his full attention. "I apologize for not being around more. I shall speak to the magistrate tomorrow and find out what recourse we have to deal with the dogs. I'm sure they were once someone's beasts and have become feral. If you permit, I'll return in a few days to discuss a plan of action. Perhaps we can resolve this problem together."

Puffing up, Mr. Green gets up from the crate where he sits talking to Gwen. He's a burly man with ruddy skin. His wife and twin sons stand, looking on from the back of the barnyard. He shakes Theo's hand, and it's a strong grip. "I appreciate you coming out to see us, Your Grace. I'm sure you have more important matters to deal with."

"None that I can think of, Mr. Green. Your family's well-being is vital for this community."

Mrs. Green grins and pushes her blond hair back into her bun. The breeze forces it back into her eyes.

Gwen stands. "It's good to see all of you. I hope to see you at the Christmas Ball next week."

"We wouldn't miss it, Miss Carter. It was very good news to hear that it would be back. We missed those parties while the duke was sick. We all prayed for him and for you when we heard he'd passed." Mrs. Green takes Gwen's offered hand and the two ladies exchange a warm look.

They walk back to the carriage and Theo helps Gwen up to the seat. Her hand is so strong, yet small and feminine. When had she become so lovely? Of course, he remembers when. She'd been sixteen and he'd returned from Oxford. He'd known for many years that his uncle wanted him to marry the duke's ward. He'd overheard the duke say as much to Theo's father. Of course, he'd only been a boy of twelve when he'd been eavesdropping. Hating that he was likely to be bullied into marrying, he rebelled, and ashamedly, Gwen had taken the brunt of that rebellion. It was inconceivable that he would marry at all, let alone the little girl who'd cried so pitifully the day she'd arrived.

After Oxford, he realized she was no longer a little girl and had a great many things to recommend her, not the least of which were beauty and brains. So, he stayed away as much as possible, and when he did show up, he was petulant and rude. After a while, it became a bad habit.

Those kinds of behavior needed breaking if he was going to be half the man his father and uncle were.

Climbing into the carriage, he takes the reins. "That was a good meeting. Thank you, Gwendolyn. It's clear that family likes you very much."

Her brows rise, wrinkling her normally smooth forehead. She opens her mouth as if she's about to comment and closes it again. Once they're underway, she says, "Would you mind stopping at the Pickering farm? I understand Mrs. Pickering is heavy with child, and I've packed some meat and bread for her and the family."

"Is that the groom's wife?"

"Yes. They married two years ago and this is their first child."

Looking at his pocket watch, he nods. "We have an appointment with a new steward at three, but we should have time for a brief visit."

A slight twist of her mouth tells him that again she wants to say something but is holding back.

"Gwendolyn, if you have something to say, feel free. I'm sure I can take any criticism you might have." He braces for whatever she's holding in. Despite his brave words, he wants her good opinion more than is natural.

Slowly she folds her hands on her lap and pulls her shoulders back. "I don't trust you, Theo. You're being very agreeable and gentlemanly, but I expect at any moment you will return to your natural state of judgmental and overbearing."

"I hope to not be that man ever again. I have already apologized. What more can I do?" His chest tightens and if not for the need to guide the horse, he would rub away that ache.

"Nothing. It makes no difference. I'll leave once you have a new steward who is up to date on all the workings of your estate. Then I see no reason for us to ever be in each other's company again. After all, it's unlikely a duke and an Everton Lady would cross paths in society." The carriage bobbles, and she grips his arm, then releases it as if he were made of hot coal.

Slowing the horse to a stop at the edge of the farm where the Pickerings live, he ties off the reins and turns on the small seat to face her. "Once, we were friends. I hope to regain your good opinion."

Worry or perhaps doubt darken her eyes. Her cheeks pinken. "I would like to believe you're sincere, but..."

"You mistrust me. I shall endeavor to make amends." Unable to stop himself, he touches her cheek. It's even softer than he imagined. "I'm not a bad person, Gwendolyn."

Eyes wide, she places her hand over his, though she doesn't push him away. Fear and longing war in her eyes.

Hope blazes inside him.

She leans in a fraction. "I suspect you're after something that I have, though I can't imagine what that might be. You've seen the books. I'm not hiding a secret key to some buried ducal treasure, Theo."

Joy floods his heart. She's delightful and adorable. "Too bad, what fun it would be to go on a treasure hunt like we did once when we were children."

A soft smile tugs at her lips and lights her eyes. "There's little time for treasure hunts once grown. It's a shame."

He'd give all his money if he thought it would keep that joy in her eyes. "Do you think you might stay through the Christmas Ball? It's my first, and I don't want to make a mess of things."

"I'll make the arrangements for the ball." She looks ahead once again.

Taking it as his cue, he urges the horse toward the Pickering house. It's a small, neat farm with a whitewashed house with a door in the center. The barn has a gated yard and several pigs, as well as a cow staring at them as they pull to a stop.

The front door opens, and a woman in her early twenties steps out, holding her full, rounded belly. When she sees Gwen, she grins and waves. "This is a nice surprise. I'd heard you'd come for a visit, Miss Carter." Catching sight of Theo, she makes a quick curtsy. "Your Grace."

Gwen rushes to her and takes her hands. "You look beautiful. Not long now and you'll be a mama."

Mrs. Pickering beams. "Mrs. Birch, the midwife, thinks it will be another two weeks. But I'm hoping for a Christmas baby."

Theo takes the basket out of the carriage and carries it to the door. "Miss Carter brought you a few things."

"That's very kind." Mrs. Pickering invites them in and offers them tea.

Declining the invitation due to the upcoming meeting with the new steward, they say their goodbyes and continue back to Crestworth House.

Lady Chervil awaits them in the office with Mr. Dunkin. She's sitting on one of the chairs, telling the tall, thin man about an adventure to Africa she had some years earlier. If the scene had been committed to canvas, the piece would have been called a comedy of opposites. As always, the lady is wearing a flowery dress with layers of flowing material. Today, the color is pale blue. She waves her hands as she says, "It was the greatest moment of my life to step off of that ship and onto the ancient land of Africa. So many people and so hot, I thought I might faint, but I was determined not to miss a moment of the day."

Mr. Dunkin didn't spare her a glance. In a dark-brown suit, he stood like a statue, staring over her shoulder. His dark hair is sparse and slicked back from his gaunt face. Lifting his long nose in the air, he gave no sign of interest in Lady Chervil's story, despite the fact that she told it with great enthusiasm. His bony hands were crossed and the only sign that he was indeed alive was the tapping of one finger on his upper arm.

Giving Gwen a glance, Theo is happy to see her amusement matches his.

The butler, Lamb, interrupts their spying. "Your Grace, Mr. Dunkin is waiting in the study."

With a push, Theo fully opens the door. "So I see. Thank you, Lamb. Will you see that the horse and carriage are put away? We left them at the front."

With only the hint of a smile, Lamb bows and leaves.

Mr. Dunkin turns to the door as if coming to attention.

"Oh, good. I fear the good sir was tiring of my stories." Mrs. Chervil laughs as she rises and goes on. "I'll leave the three of you to it, but do call if you need me."

Theo bows. "Thank you for your charming assistance, madam."

Once Lady Chervil has gone and introductions are made, Gwen goes to the desk. She pulls out the leather-bound books, six volumes in all. "This top one is the accounting. I have broken the farms down by plot size and function. The house has several accounts and is separate from the working farm on this land. I do not include the banking here as it is included with the London House."

Dunkin says nothing and stares at Gwen as if she's a three-headed hydra.

Annoyed, Theo steps to the desk and opens another drawer. "I took the liberty of bringing the London accounts with me."

Taking the one book from him, Dunkin says, "I shall look this over, Your Grace. I'm sure the other accounts will need to be completely revised to suit a real business mind. You can leave them on the desk."

Dropping the heavy volumes with a loud thud on the desk, Gwen's eyes narrow. "It seems I've been dismissed. Good afternoon." She storms out.

Oblivious, Dunkin flips pages in the banking book. He nods. "This seems in order."

Fury rises inside Theo, though even he is surprised by how angry the dismissal of Gwen's abilities as bookkeeper has made him. His fists clench at his sides. "You may be wise to rethink the woman you just dismissed since she is the one who kept those accounts. She's been keeping the ducal estates running for the last six years."

Slowly Dunkin lifts his head. "The girl? Are you certain, Your Grace? Perhaps a pretty face and a fancy story is enough to make you believe such a thing is possible. I can assure you that no girl or woman could have managed an estate of this size without leaving it in disaster."

The door is agape and there's a sharp intake of breath.

Theo's rage is barely contained. "Put that accounting book down, please. You are dismissed, Mr. Dunkin."

"I beg your pardon?" Brown eyes wide and lips pulled to a thin line, Dunkin's skin pales, which would have seemed impossible just moments ago.

"It would seem you are not a good fit for my estates. I shall pay for your travel expenses and a room at the inn for the night if you leave quietly now. If you linger, I will have you tossed on your ass by my footman and you will pay your own way home." Theo considers punching the man in the nose just for good measure but resists the urge.

With a huff, Dunkin tugs the front of his coat into place and storms out of the room.

From the foyer, Lamb says, "Good day, sir." The door closes.

Stepping from the shadow of the threshold, Gwen steps inside the study. "You sent him away." Her eyes are wide and full of confusion.

Theo's heart tightens, and he steps closer to her.

Chapter Six

G wen shouldn't have stayed by the door and eavesdropped. It had only been that she'd worked so hard to keep all of the estates running in good order and couldn't bear the idea of some hardheaded man making a mess of them. If she stayed and heard something untenable, she could talk to Theo about it later. That was it; she was there to advise the duke and that's what she would do.

Never in her wildest imagination would she have expected Theo to defend her. "You sent him away."

Theo steps closer, eyes blazing with something warm and dangerous. "He wasn't a good fit."

"Why not?" She takes a step back despite her desire to bring him closer and comes up against the door, which clicks shut.

Not stopping, Theo leans in until she has to crane her neck to look into his eyes. Why does he have to be so handsome? "Do you think I would allow anyone to speak about you that way?"

Breath coming too fast, she finds her voice. "I wouldn't have thought you'd care how anyone spoke about me."

Drawing his face close to hers, he closes his eyes. "You would have thought wrong, Gwendolyn."

All her life, she hated the way he said her full name, and he was the only one who called her that, yet at this moment, it sounds lovely. "Are you going to kiss me, Theo?"

His eyes open. "I considered it very seriously but thought you might slap my face."

Reaching up, she skims her fingers over his jaw with half a day's stubble. "It's a risk."

A half smile tugs at his mouth. "You're worth it."

As his lips meet hers, a bolt of fire and feelings rush through her. His mouth is both soft and strong.

She gasps and his tongue presses between her lips. A riot of emotions and lustful thoughts rocket through her, though none of it makes sense. Her body trembles, and her knees buckle.

Theo wraps his arm around her waist and cups her cheek, brushing his thumb over her skin and settling his hand around her neck.

Touching her tongue to his sends heat between her legs and a soft moan rises from her. She grips his shoulders, pressing her body tight to his.

Footsteps in the foyer wake her from the fog his kiss creates. Pushing on his chest ends the kiss though he doesn't move away. Instead, he presses his forehead to hers and breathes in great gulps of air. "Was this a foolish mistake, Gwendolyn?"

The warmth of his body is too good and too right. She ducks under his arm and moves away. "I think we must have been caught up in some kind of strange moment, Your Grace. I should leave you alone. I'm sure you'll be able to find a more suitable steward in a few days and in the meantime, we can plan the ball."

Still hunched and leaning his arm on the door, it takes him

a few breaths to recover enough to straighten. "Would you like to look over the guest list I've made?"

All she can think is that she needs to get away from him and clear her head. She never should have let him kiss her. He has no reason to court her, so he either intends to humiliate her or prove some point. Lifting her chin, she swallows down all the tender emotions that forced their way into her stupid head. "I'm going to my room now. If you'll leave the list on the desk, I'll come and look at it later."

When she reaches the door, he steps back so she can open it. "I know I shouldn't have kissed you, but I can't regret it, Gwendolyn."

Part of her wants to believe he kissed her because he likes her, but the greater part is sensible. Dukes don't pursue their uncle's ward and Theo Dandridge can barely stand to be in the same room with her. It's always been that way. She runs up the steps and doesn't stop until she's in her room.

For the next four days, Gwen avoids Theo and keeps Lady Chervil close. Whatever his game is, she has a job to do and he's not going to distract her. The ball is only two days away and after that, she'll return to London and he'll do whatever it is he wishes and they'll never see each other again. Why does that thought create a lump in her chest?

She's meant to go to the study to finalize the guest list, but clutching the list in her hand, she bolts into the garden and watches the snow fall lightly and cover the grass.

Ignoring the cold, she dashes a tear away. Why did he change and why now? She knew how to deal with surly and rude. But a kind and gentlemanly Theo is dangerous.

The warm soft fur of her cloak closes over her shoulders. Theo's hands remain at her neck. "You'll catch a cold."

"Thank you."

"Are you avoiding me?"

Lying isn't in her nature. "Yes."

His breath tickles her temple as he wraps his strong arms around her from behind. "Because of the kiss?"

"You are not acting normally and it's confusing. I'll be leaving in a few days. Then you can find a proper duchess, and I'll make my life as an Everton Lady. We shouldn't repeat the kiss and you shouldn't be holding me like this." The words sound like a scolding, but her voice is soft and tears are very close to the surface. She makes no move to get away from him.

His lips press against her temple. "I've wanted to kiss you for many years, Gwendolyn. I'm sorry if my acting on a long-held desire has upset you."

Her mind reels with the idea that he'd ever thought of kissing her while he behaved so atrociously. "I don't believe you. How can you have wanted to kiss me when you were constantly criticizing me for one thing or another." She pulls away from his embrace and immediately misses the warmth and comfort of his body.

"I have many flaws and should explain myself better. I don't think I knew exactly how I felt until you left, promising never to return." He looks from her to the snowy garden. "May I change the subject?"

"Please." Sorrow and relief flood her. She wants to know what explanation he could possibly have, but at the same time, is terrified of her own growing attraction to him.

"I went out this morning with several of the men from the town. We found the pack of wild dogs. They have been captured. The baker identified one as Mr. Ferrier's hound and said the man had passed a couple of years ago. There were four other dogs with him and a litter of seven pups."

Heart in her throat, Gwen's emotions over Theo are so close to the surface that she'll surely burst into tears when he tells her the dogs have been disposed of. She forces her hand away from her throat and makes a fist. "You killed them all." A tear escapes.

He cocks his head, his gaze never wavering from hers. "No. We brought them to Mr. Pickering's farm. The townsmen will try to turn them back into hunting dogs if that's possible. At the very least they'll find a home for the pups once they're weened. I've talked to Mrs. Hampton about sending scraps over to feed them. That should help keep them away from the livestock."

Gwen is full of shame for thinking the worst of him. "I'm sorry."

Shrugging, he says, "No need." His eyes show that she'd hurt him.

Mrs. Hampton calls from the back door. "Miss Carter is needed in the kitchen. Cook is beside himself over a large chicken or some such nonsense."

Maybe she should let cook rant for a while and hear everything Theo has to say. Her lack of faith in his honesty, along with outright fear, have her running as far away from him as she can. Like a coward, she runs inside and to the kitchen.

Once Gwen sorts out the party food issues, she sneaks up to her room and flops on the bed.

"What happened?" Honoria asks.

She pops up with her hand clutching her chest. "You scared the life out of me."

Honoria raises her eyebrows and stares from the chair near

the fireplace. "Quite jumpy, Gwen."

"I've just been dealing with the cook and came up for a rest." It was the truth, at least, most of it.

Honoria rises and flounces around the room, holding her white gloves in one hand and running her other hand over them. "I've noticed that you have been avoiding the duke for the last few days. I also noticed that he has been observing you with more interest and a bit of a *look* in his eyes."

"I always avoid him." Gwen crosses her arms over her chest. "What kind of look?"

Wagging her finger, Honoria shakes her head. "Not so fast. Tell me what happened between the two of you."

For the first time, Gwen thinks her inability to lie is a flaw. "The solicitor who came for the position was rude to me, and I expected Theo to take the man's part."

"But the duke sent him packing." Honoria gets a dreamy look. "Very romantic."

"I don't see it as romantic. Puzzling, but there was nothing else." Perhaps that was a bit of a fib, but more to herself than to Honoria.

"He did it because he couldn't bear to have anyone disrespect you." Coming closer, Honoria stands in front of Gwen. "Did something else happen that you should tell me about, my dear?"

Why would he care? Why does he care? What did he want to tell her before he changed the subject in the garden? Would he have told her if she'd not run like the coward she is? Gwen touches her lips, still feeling the burn of Theo's kiss from days later. "He kissed me."

A wide smile spreads across Honoria's face and she sits on the mattress. "Ah, well, that's interesting. Did he steal the kiss or were you an active participant?"

Gwen's cheeks heat. Her chest tightens and her skin tingles

with the memory of the kiss.

With a chuckle, Honoria says, "I can see from the flush in your cheeks that nothing was stolen. Perhaps you should consider why the man you thought disliked you would defend you and kiss you."

"It's all I've been able to think about. What is he after? Years of his disdain or absence and now he seems like another man." A memory forces its way into her mind. "Once, when I was seventeen, he came home from traveling abroad and he took me to a dance in town. Of course, his uncle told him to, but we danced that night and had a nice time. I thought we might become friends, but he left the next morning before I rose and we didn't see him again for two full years."

Honoria pats Gwen's hand. "Don't think about it too much. You must have a lot to do with only two days left before the Christmas Ball."

"The staff here has it all in hand. Another candidate for steward is coming tomorrow morning. His name is Mr. Geldman. His resume is very impressive. We'll stay for the party and leave in time to be back in London for Christmas. Do you have a family to spend the day with?" Gwen fusses with a loose thread on her skirt. Perhaps one of the maids can mend it.

Sauntering to the door, Honoria looks over her shoulder. "I've been married a few times, my dear. I have many family members who will host me if we return to London, but they are quite used to my independence as well. You should get that rest you came in for and put all of the questions out of your mind. A smart woman like you will make the right decisions when the time comes.

"What decisions?"

Honoria leaves without responding.

With a sigh, Gwen lies on the mattress, though she fails to put Theo out of her mind.

Chapter Seven

It's late and Theo can't sleep. His mind is filled with plots and plans to win Gwen's friendship. He owes that much to his uncle. Even if he can't change her mind about The Everton Domestic Society, she should know she always has his friendship to call upon.

His stomach clenches with thoughts of her leaving again. His behavior toward Gwen over the years is his greatest regret. He might have just explained to her that he didn't wish to marry, and that his uncle wanted to push them together.

Giving up on sleep, he goes toward the kitchen in search of a snack. Light coming through from under the library door gives him pause. It was unheard of for Lamb to forget to put out a lantern. With a sigh, he opens the library door.

A single candle flickers in its holder on the long table. Looking from one end of the dim library to the other, Theo sees nothing but shadows.

"You're letting in a draft. Close the door if you're coming in." Gwen's voice cuts through his thoughts.

The candle flickers wildly to prove her point and sends a cascade of shadows around the floor-to-ceiling bookshelves.

Theo closes the door as ordered and then rounds the back of the sofa. "What are you doing here?"

She sits up and grips the small lap blanket to her chin which exposes her bare feet and legs. "Theo. I thought it must be Lamb or Mrs. Hampton checking on the light."

"The staff has gone to bed. Why are you awake?" Trying not to stare at her bare calves or notice how shapely they are is impossible.

Seeing the direction of his gaze, she gasps and pulls her feet up so that she's balled up under the blanket with only the frilly bottom of her nightgown showing. "I couldn't sleep so I came down to read, but my eyes got tired so I thought I'd rest them a moment. Why are you here?"

Theo sits on the overstuffed chair adjacent to her and leans his elbows on his knees. "I couldn't sleep either. I may have offended you in the garden today and that was not my intention."

She lowers the blanket an inch. "I wasn't offended, only confused."

"I wanted to explain my behavior." He rubs the back of his neck, hoping stalling will give him time to find the right words.

"Which behavior are you going to explain, Theo?" She drops the shield, exposing the adorable white nightgown that covers her almost completely.

"I beg your pardon?"

"Are you going to tell me why you're pretending to like me after years of being clear that you do not, or do you plan to explain why you don't like me and treated me as an annoyance for the last eighteen or so years?" She cocks her head.

The way her neck is exposed makes him want to bury his nose in the crook of her shoulder and breathe in all the essence of Gwendolyn. It's not possible to keep himself from wanting her, so he just pushes that desire aside. "I have always liked you very much."

"I know that is not true." She clearly has no idea how her indignation pushes her breasts forward, or how much the resulting posture makes his mouth water.

Lord, but she's the most adorable woman he's ever seen. How had it taken him so long to consider acting on what he's known since she stopped being a girl and became a woman? "Gwendolyn, I liked you from the moment you came to my uncle, weeping and alone." He holds up a hand to stop whatever she's about to say, even though he can't keep his gaze away from her soft sweet lips. "I know it may not have always seemed that way, but it's true."

"You told me once that I was an interloper with no business in your family." Her voice cracks slightly.

Cringing at the memory of having said exactly those words, he takes a deep breath and grips his hands together to steel his courage. "I was twelve the Christmas when I said that. It was the day after I'd jumped in the cold pond and gotten punished. I sneaked down the steps later that night to see how bad my penance would be."

"You'd scared your mother half to death." Gwen tries to hide her smile.

"I'll tell you a secret. I still jump in that pond every year in the cold. It's quite invigorating. I just make sure no one is around to scold me." He laughs.

Wrapping her arms around herself, she shivers. "It sounds dreadful. What happened when you were twelve and you were snooping?"

"My father was in the study with my uncle and they were saying how I was wild, but one day when I married you, I would calm down."

She gasps and covers her mouth with her hand. "I was only seven and they were already marrying me off."

"Imagine how I felt as a boy of twelve not having any choices. I thought if you hated me, they couldn't force me to do anything. Uncle doted on you so much, I knew he'd never make you do anything you were opposed to. My goal was to make you hate me." Shame washes over him at having done too good a job.

"You never succeeded, Theo. I hated what you said and often your behavior, which I didn't understand, but I could never hate you. In the back of my mind, there was still the boy who'd played with me when I was scared and alone." A tear rolls down her cheek.

Theo drops to his knees and takes her hand. Staring into her green eyes, he's lost in how soulful and beautiful she is. Every moment spent with this woman should have been treasured. Instead, he'd been an ass. "I pray that's true. I truly do. After a few years, it became a bad habit. Admittedly, I still love to see you in a temper. Your eyes flash with fire and your cheeks turn bright red. You're beautiful."

Pulling her hands from his, she smiles and slaps his hand. "That's just silly."

"Why is it silly?" Her mouth is only a few inches away. He could lean forward and kiss her, and he longs for that kiss.

"Because you don't want to marry me now any more than you did at twelve. You're not courting me." Her voice catches at the end and another tear rolls free. She dashes it away.

Cupping her cheek, he brushes his lips across hers. "I would court you, Gwendolyn. I would make a fool of myself for you."

"And then what?" Her eyes close and she drifts forward as if longing for his lips as much as he longs for hers.

"May I kiss you?"

"You just did." She threads her fingers through his hair.

Breathing in her warm floral scent, he runs his mouth along her neck, pulls free the bow at her throat, then kisses along her collarbone. "I need more of you, Gwendolyn."

She arches toward him. "How much more?" With her other hand, she traces a path down the back of his arm, then up again.

It's a gentle caress, but his cock jumps to attention. "All. I will settle for nothing less than all of you." He pushes her nightgown down her shoulders, freeing one perfect breast. Lowering his mouth, he sucks her nipple.

A soft cry rises, and she arches her back for more. "Theo, I need..."

"What do you need?" His body is on fire for her. Longing to kiss every inch of soft skin, he makes his way to her other breast and licks and sucks until they're both panting, and the scent of her arousal fills the library.

"More," she whispers. "I need more."

"Let me take you to my bed."

She's going to say no. He might have gotten her to lie with him here, but she shouldn't be taken on a settee where all the servants will know by morning. Gwen is a lady and should be shown all the pleasure of his regard. Waiting for her to slap him or scream for help is all he can do. Wanting her is unstoppable, but needing her to want him is a dream.

"Yes." She clutches his head. "I need more. We can have this and no one will ever know."

She said yes. The rest of what she assumes is an argument for later, but in this moment, her desire outweighs all the good sense rushing around that brilliant pretty head of hers. Sliding his arms under her back and legs, he scoops her up.

Stopping briefly to blow out the candle, he bolts for the door and up the steps. Painfully hard, he has to go slower than he'd like. The most surprising thing is how intimate it is to have

Gwen in his arms with her head resting on his chest. She trusts him despite all he's done and how he's treated her.

Heart racing, he pushes through the door and into the large bedroom newly cleaned and rearranged for him after his uncle's death. Gently, he rests her on the mattress, following to lie beside her.

"Theo, I feel very strange. I need you to touch me." She closes her eyes and blushes bright red.

Touching her knee still covered in the cotton gown, he draws her leg toward him. "Where do you wish to be touched, sweetheart?"

She traces a path between her breasts, pushing the nightgown down until it bunches at her hips. Slipping her hand beneath the material, she moans. "Here."

"You will drive me mad, Gwendolyn." He presses his shaft against her thigh looking for some relief, but only making his need grow. Lifting to his knees, he admires her half-naked form. "You're very beautiful."

She opens her eyes as if checking to see if he's sincere. "I'd like to see you as well."

Standing, Theo strips out of his shirt.

Gwen rises to her elbows and watches his every move. Her pupils are dilated as she blushes and studies him.

He removes his breeches and stands before her, hoping she won't run. "Are you sorry you asked, because your eyes are wide with obvious shock."

Shaking her head, she looks away from his erection and shifts her gaze to his eyes. "I've never seen a man naked before. You're very beautiful, Theo."

"I'm glad you think so. May I remove your nightgown and ease your need?" He runs his fingers along the soft skin of her ankle.

With her gaze still locked on his, she nods.

Taking half a step closer, he leans in to grip the fabric at her hips and slides it down her strong, satiny legs, letting it fall to the floor in a pillow of white. Kneeling at the side of the bed, he grips her thighs and draws her to the edge of the mattress. Breathing deep her warm sensual scent, his cock jerks painfully. His need will have to wait. Right now, her desire is all he cares about.

Still watching him, eyes as wide as saucers, she parts her lips as if to speak.

Theo slides his tongue between her folds. She's as sweet as the most precious honey. He moans.

On a gasp, she lies back and threads her fingers through his hair. "Theo, that's... Oh, god."

Licking and sucking her center until she's writhing with her coming orgasm, he's so aroused he may erupt along with her. Determined not to let that happen, he wills his desire down while reveling in her pleasure. Needing to feel the moment, he slips his finger inside her tight sheath.

Her body clasps around his digit as she comes apart. Biting her bottom lip to keep the house from hearing her, she tries to pull her center away from his mouth.

"You're perfect. I'm a fool for not telling you sooner." Wrapping his arms around her, he brings them both to the middle of the bed.

Chapter Eight

Nothing can ever compare to the pleasure Theo's mouth produces. Gwen's body quakes and shivers with the aftershock of the beautiful moment when she crashed into a million pieces. In his arms, she slowly regains her wits. "I had no idea."

"The real miracle is that you can do that again if you wish." His smile lights his eyes, but not as if he's prideful. He looks smitten, but that cannot be.

"Can I?" Excitement builds in her chest and sensations stir again between her legs and low in her belly. Glancing at his shaft, her cheeks heat. "And can I give you pleasure as well?"

He caresses her cheek and pushes her hair from her face. "Not this night, sweetheart. Tonight is about you."

Having left herself so vulnerable had been a mistake. Of course, he doesn't want to leave himself in the same position. Her chest tightens painfully. "I should go." She sits up, then jumps from the bed, grabbing her nightgown from the floor. "This was..." Part of her wants to say it was a mistake, but she can't bring herself to utter those words. She drags the cotton over her head and ties the bow at her throat.

Theo gapes at her. "You're leaving?"

"I must. If I were caught here, it would be terrible for both of us. Lady Chervil would insist you marry me." A nervous laugh bubbles up while she forces her tears down.

Moving to the edge of the mattress, he puts on his shirt, which covers him to the middle of his thick muscular thighs. "I wish you wouldn't look so aghast, Gwendolyn. What we shared was, in my mind, quite beautiful. Whatever you think it means, you should talk to me about."

Tears are fighting to get out. She backs toward the door. "It doesn't mean anything. You found a woman alone in the library. I behaved like a wanton. These things happen all the time and no one needs to know about it." Her voice cracks on the last few words.

Standing, he steps toward her. "Don't leave."

Gwen opens the door. "Good night. I'll be leaving Crestworth after the ball. Don't trouble yourself about me, Your Grace. I have a solid plan for my future." She rushes out the door. Blinding tears fill her eyes as she finds her way to her own room where she bolts the door and throws herself into the bed.

What a fool she'd been to think he had feelings for her. No. She never really believed that. He wants to keep her around due to some sense of duty. She's a grown woman and can take care of herself. Tonight was a strange set of circumstances that will never happen again.

She cries harder into her pillow.

Unable to look Theo in the eyes, Gwen keeps her focus on Mr. Robert Geldman. "You will find all the books in order." She shows the candidate for steward how she noted each farm.

"I see, Miss Carter. This is very efficient." Mr. Geldman is in his early thirties with straight dark hair and brown eyes. Tall and thin, he has a pleasing manner and shows no sign that he's put off by a woman showing him the accounts.

"I have kept separate accounts for each of the estates, but the assets are listed in this volume." She opens the book and points to the lines. "You'll see here that those assets associated with Crestworth are marked with a C and Treadmore with a T. Everything is coded this way and at the front of the book is a legend to reference if you're unsure."

Theo says nothing. He sits behind the desk, toying with the edge of one of the books but making eye contact with no one. His shoulders are hunched and his expression unreadable.

Gwen looks away.

Clearing his throat, Mr. Geldman turns to Theo. "Would you mind if I studied these for a few minutes, Your Grace? I may have questions for you or Miss Carter."

Standing, Theo says, "By all means. I'm sure I will be of little use to you, but as you've seen, Miss Carter is an expert on the matter." His gaze lands on Gwen for a long second.

She'd swear she saw pain in his stark blue eyes, but she must be mistaken.

"I'll give you all the time you need. Let Lamb know when you need me." He strides from the study with a nod to Mr. Geldman.

Staring after him, Mr. Geldman cocks his head. "Did I say something that offended him, miss?"

Gwen shakes her head. "No. I think he quite likes you, sir."

"Really?" He turns to her. "May I ask why you don't take this job through The Everton Domestic Society? You certainly know your way around accounting."

With a sigh, Gwen flops into one of the chairs in front of the desk. "It would be like moving backward, if you take my meaning, Mr. Geldman. I need to start a new life. Besides, I don't know if Mrs. Chervil will wish to chaperone indefinitely."

"I would very much like this position, so I won't argue your points, though there is quite a bit to refute." His grin reveals straight white teeth and kind eyes.

"I think I shall be sorry you and I don't have time to become good friends."

They spend the next hour going over each ledger one by one until Mr. Geldman is well acquainted with her system and thoroughly impressed by her keen mind.

G wen finds Theo sitting in the freezing garden surrounded by snow. She steels herself against her softer feelings for him and his undeniable good looks. His broad shoulders stiffen as she approaches.

"What is your opinion, Gwendolyn?" None of the warmth from the other night exists in the way he says her name.

She stands several feet away, gripping her coat closed. "Mr. Robert Geldman has a sharp mind and his mathematical skills are far beyond mine. He's well-educated and very pleasant. If I were you, I would hire him."

He nods. "Is everything in order for the Christmas Ball?"

Her throat clogs. He isn't quite as cold with her as in the days before his uncle died, but all the warmth and friendship are gone. Her throat closes, but she squeaks out, "Yes."

Jerking his head to look at her, he narrows his eyes. "Are

you upset because of what happened the other night or is it something else?"

"I'm not upset." But her tight voice betrays the lie.

Those full beautiful lips twitch and he almost smiles. "You're a terrible liar, Gwendolyn."

"I know. I just don't want to talk to you about my feelings, Theo." Despite wanting to run as fast as she can back to the house, her feet remain rooted to the snowy path.

A long sigh causes his shoulders to slump. "I wish you would reconsider leaving Crestworth. Give me time to show you I'm not the monster you think I am."

"I don't think you're a monster. I'm confused by so much change so suddenly." She bites the inside of her cheek to keep herself from saying more.

Theo stands. "I'm sorry. I deserve that. I'll go and inform, Mr. Geldman that he has the position if he wants it. I'm sure that if you approve him, he is well qualified. I'll see you at dinner?"

Unable to bear sitting with him through a meal and wondering what he's thinking about her, she takes the cowardly way out. "I'm quite tired. I think I'll take a small meal in my room."

He nods his head once and looks at her as if he knows exactly why she's "tired" and says, "Then I'll see you at the ball tomorrow."

Those damn tears that are always so close to the surface lately push through her emotions. "Yes. Of course." She runs past him to the house, up the stairs, and heads for her room.

Lady Chervil is floating down the hall toward her. "What on earth is wrong, Gwen?"

"I'm a fool." She goes around Honoria and gets into her room in time to bury her tears in her pillow.

The door opens and closes with a soft snick. The mattress shifts as Honoria sits and rubs her palm over Gwen's back.

For twenty minutes Gwen cries and Honoria says nothing.

As her sobs turn to hiccups, Honoria hands her a handkerchief. "You should wash your face, dearest."

Feeling wrung out, Gwen pushes herself from the bed and does as she's told. She scrubs her face in the cold water from the basin until her cheeks sting. While she dries her face, another sob tries to take her, but she pushes it away. She gets back on the mattress and stares up at the ceiling. "I'll be fine now. Thank you for comforting me."

"You would feel better if you told me what's wrong." Honoria lies back on the mattress next to her with her hands steepled like someone in their coffin.

"I've done a stupid foolish thing." Again, she has to push down the sob.

"I'm sure whatever it is, it can be remedied." Her voice is soft and comforting. It reminds Gwen of how her mother spoke when she fell from a fence and skinned her palm.

The familiarity makes Gwen want to confide in Honoria. She hasn't had a mother figure in her life since she was five. "You are the kindest person."

"No. I just like you." Honoria looks at Gwen and smiles.

Impossibly, Gwen giggles, lifting a bit of the dread building in her gut. But then the truth rolls back into place. "I've fallen in love with him." A tear streams down her cheek.

Honoria turns fully toward her and wipes the tear away with her handkerchief. "I suppose *him* is Theo Dandridge?"

With a nod, Gwen swallows more sobs.

"I don't think that's anything to cry about, dearest. Do you think His Grace shares your feelings?"

"Of course not. He doesn't even like me. He just thinks his

uncle would want him to be my guardian. I don't want to be anyone's duty for the rest of my life. And then what? In a year when he's had enough of my constantly being underfoot, he'll marry me off to some horrible sod? No. I can make my own decisions." Despite her building anger, more tears stream down her cheeks.

Honoria shakes her head and sits up. "You should ask him for his true feelings instead of deciding you know them. Perhaps you would be surprised. I sincerely doubt the Duke of Stratham would be inclined to marry you off to anyone, sod or gentleman."

"Why not? Am I that undesirable? Would I be a terrible wife? Of course, I would. I never know when to act the part of a simpleton." Gwen punches the mattress.

"The answer to that is, never. However, I don't believe His Grace is offended or bothered by your obvious intelligence." She pats Gwen's hand. "Get some rest, dearest. I'll have a plate sent up with your dinner."

"Thank you, Lady Chervil. You are very kind to me." She closes her eyes. Why couldn't she have made Papa understand that she was grown? Why had she been so hesitant to find a suitable husband? If she'd been a normal lady of the ton, she'd have insisted on a new wardrobe and a season or two in town, but she'd been content to stay home and keep the books. She'd never considered a different life until it was too late. This was all her fault.

Chapter Nine

T he Christmas Ball cannot begin until the duke starts the dancing. Theo shakes hands with Mr. Green and several other neighbors. It's the one night that farmers, the butcher, and the local gentry all gather together as equals. Theo's uncle, at Gwen's urging, felt it was important to be one community and get to know each other.

She was right, of course. Men were more likely to help each other in tough times when they'd taken a meal together, drank, and danced together.

The orchestra tunes their instruments while he searches the ballroom for the only woman he wants to hold in his arms.

Honoria grins happily and angles her head toward the French doors at the back of the room.

Weaving through the crowd and saying hello to as many people as he can, Theo spots Gwen standing in a corner like a wallflower.

When she sees him, she shrinks back. Even avoiding him, she's the most stunning sight. Her green gown flows over her curves, dipping low at her breasts. A red ribbon just under those delectable globes makes his mouth water. Her ruby hair is curled into several ringlets that frame her face and the rest flows softly over her shoulders, driving his need to run his fingers through her locks.

"Gwendolyn, why are you hiding at your own party?" He crowds her, taking in her soft floral scent.

"I'm just staying out of the way. It's your party, Your Grace." There's a shyness in her voice and posture that he doesn't like one bit.

"No. This party was created by you when you were just a girl. You told my uncle to bring the area together, and he did this for you because it was and is a brilliant idea." He forces his tone softer. "However, the ball cannot begin until we dance, so will you do me the honor of the first dance, Miss Carter?" He offers her his hand.

With a short hesitation, she accepts his hand and they walk through the crowd, which parts as they pass to the dance floor.

The conductor taps his baton.

Silence falls before the first strains of a waltz begin.

Tightening his hold on her, he steps them into the dance.

The ballroom erupts into applause before other couples surround them and join the waltz.

"I didn't think you'd want to dance with me. There are quite a few beautiful women of means here tonight." She stares at his chin as if looking him in the eyes will break some spell. He wants whatever is keeping her at arm's length to be pushed away or banished or whatever one does to remove a bad spell.

"While I'm obligated to dance with many of the women in this room, there is only one I want to hold in my arms." He hesitates, but she'll leave tomorrow and there are things he needs to say. If his pride hadn't gotten in the way he would have spoken to her yesterday. "I wish you would meet me later so we can talk, Gwendolyn. Is that too much to ask of you? I know you want to go back to London and your Society, but will you talk to me before you leave?" His heart pounds so hard, he can't remember a time he'd ever been so nervous.

An adorable crease forms between her eyes as she thinks about what he's said. Maybe he's just hoping she's thinking about it. Perhaps she just trying not to make a scene when she tells him a resounding no.

Her silence creates an awkwardness he detests. "Everyone but Mr. and Mrs. Pickering are here. I had a note earlier today that the baby would be arriving at any moment and they would not be able to come. I suppose the midwife has also missed the party."

Warmth spreads over Gwen's face making her even more beautiful. "How lovely that she'll get her Christmas baby after all."

"She has a few hours left." The ballroom is polished to a high shine and all the candles of the chandelier glitter. Green garland is draped along the wainscotting and two enormous mantels. "The ballroom looks perfect. Thank you."

"The staff did all the work." She blushes.

He shakes his head. "You made this party happen and I am grateful."

As the music draws to an end, she meets his gaze. "After the house has retired for the evening, I will come to speak to you, but only because it is *not* too much to ask after so many years of acquaintance."

The music ends, she curtsies, then walks away.

It's impossible not to laugh at her calling him an acquaintance while his mind is preoccupied with the wonderful noises she made as she came apart in his bed.

The next song begins, and he's required to dance with one of a dozen women whose mothers wish to ensnare him.

It's late and Theo sits in his study waiting for the house to take to their beds. There's no way Gwen will come to him until she believes no one will know.

At nearly five in the morning, his heart sinks. She's not coming. His urge to go to her room and lay out his feelings is so strong it takes all his will to continue staring out the window into the darkness.

Finally, he gives up and makes his way to his bedroom. The fire is lit as is to be expected, but something in the air is different as he enters. Scanning the room, his heart pounds a staccato beat as his gaze lands on Gwen sitting in the center of his mattress.

Approaching the bed, he's afraid if he moves too fast, she'll disappear. "You're here."

No longer in her gown, she's swathed in layers of white cotton, both nightgown and wrap. Her hair shines in the fire-light. "You said you wanted to talk."

"I thought we would talk in the study." He sits gingerly on the edge of the bed. His cock already fully alert to the woman of his greatest desire being in his bed.

"Should I leave?"

"No," he says too loud and too quickly. "No. I want you to stay."

A soft smile warms her face. "I think the ball was a success. Everyone seemed happy."

"Yes." He runs the back of his fingers from her wrist to her shoulder. "I wish I could have danced with you all night rather than the silly women who want only one thing from me."

"They are only doing what they were raised to do. You're a duke now. There will be women begging for your attention until you choose one of them to become your wife." She stares at the fire and the flames shimmer in her eyes.

"What if they are not who I want? What if I want a different kind of life?" His heart pounds so hard, it's a wonder she can't hear it.

"You're a duke. I suppose you can do whatever you like. A wife and a few mistresses wouldn't be given a second look by society." She keeps her attention on the fire with her hands folded in her lap.

"That is not who I am, Gwendolyn. I know you think the worst of me, but if you would give me time, I would prove to you that I am a gentleman." He'd traveled the world and met with thieves and highwaymen, yet this was the most afraid he'd ever been.

Finally, she turns and looks him in the eye. "I'm leaving tomorrow. I don't know what the rest of my life will look like, but tonight, I'd like to be in your arms. No talk. No telling each other about the past. I just want you to hold me and make me feel good. I want to make you feel good. One night, Theo. Can you give that to me?"

He would give her the world, the moon, and the sun if she asked it of him. This was more than he deserved. Standing, he strips out of his clothes and tosses them aside before lying on the bed, his arms open for her.

Getting to her feet in the center of the mattress, she lets her wrap and nightgown puddle at her feet.

No man could look at her and not think her a goddess. Tomorrow, he will tell her everything and beg her for her hand. Tonight, he'll give her what she asks for.

Pulling her into his arms, he presses his lips to hers. Sucking her top lip between his, and then the bottom. When she touches her tongue to his, he groans and pulls her tighter, pressing his knee between her thighs.

She arches her hips to rub her center against his leg.

He caresses down her back until he reaches the swell of her soft bottom.

The gentle touch of her fingers on his chest drives him mad with desire. She traces circles as she explores his abdomen and then lower, touching the tip of his shaft.

He gasps, then moans as she wraps her small hand around him. Pressing his hand over hers, he guides her up and down as their hips clash in an ancient dance.

Panting as her center finds the friction she needs, she says his name against his lips.

With a shift of his weight, he eases her back onto the mattress and slips his fingers between her slick folds, teasing her most sensitive pearl until her body arches off the bed. The scent of her arousal mixed with the soft florals he always associates with Gwen is a thing of his fondest dreams.

She cries his name on a long keen as she comes apart.

Unable to resist, he slips a finger inside her to feel her orgasm pulse. Lifting his fingers to his mouth he tastes the sweet nectar, then kisses Gwen so she can know how good it is to love her into pleasure.

As he makes to move away so she can return to her bed, she clutches his shoulder. "No. I want to give you the same pleasure."

The knot in his chest tightens. "Are you sure?"

"Please, Theo. One night is all I ask." The fact that she's begging is ridiculous.

How can she not know that he would do anything for her and that this is so much more than he deserves?

Covering her body with his, he gently spreads her thighs. Gazes locked, he kisses her slowly, making love to her mouth. He presses small kisses to her cheek, her nose, and her chin. "This may hurt for a moment, sweetheart. But only for a moment and then never again. Afterward, there will only be pleasure."

She nods and her eyes glow with a mix of passion and fear.

Wishing he could take this pain for her, he notches at her sweet core and presses forward until he meets resistance.

Gwen gasps and closes her eyes tight.

"Look at me, love." With his weight on his forearms, he brushes his finger across her cheek.

Eyes open like the warrior queen she is, she stares into his eyes.

He thrusts through.

A short cry escapes her, along with one tear.

It takes a herculean effort to stay still while her body adjusts to him. Capturing the tear on his finger, he kisses her. "Tell me when the pain eases." There's no hiding the strain in his voice. His body wants to move more than breathe.

"I want you to move, Theo." Her fingers dig into his back.

Easing out, he presses in again and they both moan. Thrusting again and again, his body is on fire with so much wanting and waiting, that it takes an effort to be patient and wait for her pleasure. It's only his desperation to see her come and hear her cry his name that holds him back.

She wraps her leg around his, allowing him to push deeper. Her moans and cries are like the finest symphony in his ears. "Theo. Oh, Theo." Her core pulses around him as her nails bite into his flesh.

The base of his spine tingles and his legs shake. As soon as her pleasure ebbs, he thrusts hard and fast before pulling out and spilling his seed between their sweat-slicked bodies.

Pressing kisses to her face, he whispers words of love.

She smiles softly. "That was much better than women say. I wonder why no one speaks of the pleasure."

"You're adorable." He laughs. "It's all men speak of."

Shifting away earns him a mumbled complaint. He caresses her cheek. "I'm just going to get a cloth to clean us up, love. I'm not leaving you." He would never leave her, but he wouldn't talk of forever now. Tomorrow, when they are both clearheaded, he will ask her to marry him.

Once he cleans them both, he wraps his arms around her and breathes in the warm scent of Gwen. "You are the most spectacular woman, Gwendolyn."

"Thank you for tonight." She sighs.

Chapter Ten

It's nearly eleven o'clock when Theo wakes to an empty bed. He searches the room, but he's alone.

Once washed and dressed, he walks down the hall to knock on Gwen's door and make sure she is all right. The door is open, the room empty, and a maid is cleaning.

"Where is Miss Carter?" His voice is harsher than he intends.

Ella, the maid, is a girl of perhaps sixteen. Brown curls push out of her white bonnet and her gray eyes are wide as she gives a trembling reply, "The ladies left almost an hour ago, Your Grace."

"Left?" He lets the word swirl around his mind. It's not possible.

Ella nods. "To London, sir."

Storming down to the foyer, Theo calls, "Lamb!"

After a moment, the butler appears from the servants' door under the stairs. "Your Grace?"

"Why did you let her leave?" Theo paces around the large, round table in the foyer. The urge to smash something is strong, but he spares the vase filled with hothouse roses. "I need my horse."

Lamb cocks his head. "The ladies had always planned to return to London today. You didn't mention that you'd like for them to stay longer. I assumed you made your goodbyes at the ball last night."

His panic is acute. How could she think he wanted her to leave before he woke? He calms his mind. "I need my horse, Lamb."

"Of course, Your Grace." Lamb signals for the footman standing near the front door. "Joe, please go and inform the groom that His Grace needs his horse saddled and brought to the front."

Joe runs to do as he's told.

"Your Grace?" Robert Geldman's calm voice and demeanor are incongruous with how Theo feels. He looks around, taking in the mood and situation. "I see that you're in a hurry, sir, but I noticed something in an old ledger, and I think you'll want to see it right away."

"Is it that important?" It takes an effort not to snipe, but his voice still comes out annoyed.

Robert clears his throat. "Um, if you're going after Miss Carter, you will wish to know this first, Your Grace. It concerns her."

With a sigh and the knowledge that Gwen will be at Everton House, Theo looks at Lamb. "Hold off on my horse, please."

Lamb bows.

"Show me what you've found, Mr. Geldman." They retire to the study.

E verton House seems very quiet compared to Crestworth and Gwen paces her room. She should have said goodbye, but she didn't want him to talk her out of leaving. Theo might have felt obligated to marry her after their night together and that is not what she wants.

Right?

Why can't she stop thinking about him and the way he looked at her?

A knock at her door startles her. "Yes?"

Gray opens the door but stays in the hallway. "You have a visitor, Miss Carter. I've asked him to wait in the front parlor."

Heart in her throat, Gwen says, "Who is it?"

"The gentleman just said his name is Geldman and that he is an acquaintance of yours."

"How strange. I'll go right down. Thank you, Gray." She rushes to get her notes about all of the Stratham accounts. "I'm sure he just has some questions. They must be very urgent for him to have come all this way. He could have written."

Gray stands aside and waits for her to exit the bedroom. "I also took the liberty of informing Mrs. Chervil that her services would be needed."

Heading downstairs, Gwen is surprised when Robert Geldman is waiting at the bottom of the stairs. She shakes his hand. "Was the parlor not to your liking, sir?"

"I wanted to speak to you before you went in."

Confused but not wishing to make Robert uncomfortable, Gwen says, "All right. Was there a problem with the records?"

He shakes his head. "I looked back at the books from before you began keeping the estates. I found recordings of an account that was not brought forward into the more recent books. I came to London with the duke to verify that those funds were indeed still available."

Theo is in London. Her brain tries to process what Robert is saying while not panicking over the fact that Theo is in the city. "It must be a great deal of money to have brought you both back from the country."

Robert opens his mouth, but before he can respond, the parlor door opens.

"Indeed," Theo says. "It is a great sum of money long forgotten." His hair is slightly windblown and his expression is warm with a bit of worry in his bright blue eyes.

The sight of him has her heart thrumming like a racehorse. "Your Grace." She curtsies.

"Come and sit down." Honoria's voice wafts from the parlor. "It's not good to speak of business in the foyer."

Taking a deep breath, Gwen walks past Theo without looking at him. She tries to calm herself. Whatever he's doing here it's about some bank account and not anything romantic or dramatic. She walks to the pianoforte and taps the cover in a fast beat that mimics her pulse. "What is this about a bank account that I missed and how can I help?"

When she turns, both men are standing in front of chairs adjacent to the sofa where Honoria sits drinking tea.

They won't sit unless she does so, she reins in her nerves, strides over, and sits next to Honoria.

The men sit.

Leaning his elbows on his knees, Theo says, "I'm sorry to call without sending word. We came directly from the bank. I think it might be best if Mr. Geldman explains."

Robert takes a ledger out of his briefcase and hands it to Gwen. "This is the account. It has its own books. For many years, while you were quite young, it was included with the estate. About fifteen years ago, the fifth duke separated the funds."

Opening the leather book, Gwen reads the large sum at the

bottom. "Why would he remove this from the rest of the estate?"

"If you'll turn to the front page, Miss Carter." Robert leans over and flips the page back for her.

Written in Alden Dandridge's hand in the center of the page is, *Gwendolyn Carter Estate.*

"What is the meaning of this?" Gwen's throat is dry.

Honoria whistles. "I think it means you are a very wealthy woman, my dear."

"Why would he never have told me? Where did all of this come from?" Gwen looks from Robert to Theo.

Shoulders straight and gaze soft, Theo shrugs. "I'm sure it was left to you by your parents. Perhaps my uncle worried that if you knew, you might leave him."

"I never could have. I loved him. He knew I loved him like a father." Tears stream down her cheeks.

Robert clears his throat. "I shall wait in the foyer should you need anything." He gets up and quietly leaves the parlor.

Dashing away her tears, Gwen draws a shaking breath. "You could have put all of this into a letter, Your Grace. There was no need to travel all this way."

His eyes close for a long moment and anger flashes in them when they open. "I would have come with or without the money, Gwendolyn. I was about to chase you down on horseback when Mr. Geldman came to me with this new information." Standing, he runs his finger through his hair, and paces. "Then, I had to come by coach to accommodate Mr. Geldman, and we had to verify the value of your estate."

"Why are you here?" Gwen demands, her nails biting into the palms of her hands.

"Because if you had stayed to say goodbye, I would have asked you to marry me." It's more shout than explanation.

Honoria sighs. "That could have been more romantic." She

rises and picks up the tray of biscuits and tea. "I will be in the office. Perhaps Mr. Geldman would like some tea."

Once they are alone, silence fills every space in the room.

Gwen recovers first. "I did not spend the night with you to trap you into marriage."

"Gwendolyn, I am not trapped. I wouldn't have made love with you if I hadn't intended to marry you." His jaw ticks and he rubs the back of his neck, which he often does when he expects a scolding.

"Then why would you want to marry me? For most of my life, we have been enemies. Now you return and woo me as if you care. What am I to believe?"

Kneeling on the floor, he takes her hands. "We were never enemies. I was a foolish boy and then an even stupider young man who didn't want to be told whom he should marry. I was certain that my father and uncle were trying to tame me and take away my freedom."

"Is that why you ran around town and the continent?" Gwen tries to pull her hands away.

He holds fast and rubs her palms where she made nail marks. "Honestly, I think I did it so they would see I wasn't good enough for you. Then my father died, and I didn't know how to change. I'd been playing the rake for so long."

"Now that I have the funds to make my own way in the world, you want to marry me, and then I will have nothing again." Pain radiates from the center of her chest. Loving him while he merely wants her for a prize is too horrible.

He grips her hands tighter. "Gwendolyn, look at me."

There's little choice, so she stares into those mesmerizing eyes.

His pupils dilate. "I will never touch one cent of that money. It's understandable that you will think I would chase you for your money. But if I'd wanted to, I could have kept the money a secret. Mr. Geldman is in my employ, and he would have done as I said. However, I want to marry you and, God help me, I long for you to *want* to marry me." He draws a long breath. "I love you, Gwendolyn. If there is any chance that you return my feelings, I will spend all my days endeavoring to make you happy."

She never believed he would love her or tell her. Now her mind reels with her own heart's desire. "I do love you, Theo." She stops his attempt to hug her with a hand to his chest. "I won't be bullied."

"I'm well aware. I have no desire to return to our old ways." His crooked smile is too alluring.

"If I were to marry you, all my assets would become yours. You say you don't want my money, but the law already will have given it to you." None of that is his fault, but she can't help her anger at the situation.

"It occurred to me that you might not like that. I can have Mr. Geldman put the funds in a trust that only you can access. You could start a charity, or save the funds for our children, or do some other clever thing, but I promise you, I will never touch that money for myself or the estates of the Duke of Stratham." He sits beside her. "Marry me, Gwen."

Joy floods her as if she's a girl again and he's the knight who saved her from despair. "I prefer the way you say Gwendolyn."

"Tell me?" With his heart in his eyes, he looks vulnerable and it's something she never thought she'd see from him.

"I will marry you, Theo. I love you." Anything more she might have wanted to say is quashed by his lips and embrace.

The door swings open. "I'm so happy!" Honoria wafts in with her arms outstretched. She pulls Gwen into a hug and then pats Theo's cheek. "I knew the two of you would find your way."

Jane stands in the doorway, dabbing the corners of her eyes.

That small move is the only sign of emotion from the usually stoic lady of the house. "You can be married from Everton House if you wish, Miss Carter."

"Thank you." Gwen had never had women in her life. Now she had a kind of family and knew The Everton Domestic Society would be here for her always.

Taking her hand, Theo leads her to the front window next to the pianoforte. "You have made me very happy. I never really believed you could be mine."

"Why not?" She touches his cheek, then realizes they have company and lowers her hand.

"I suppose I believed all along that I was not good enough for you, my sweet Gwendolyn." With that admission, he keeps his eyes cast to the floor.

Touching his cheek again, despite the audience, she says, "I never believed that. I only thought you disliked me."

Meeting her gaze, he says, "No. I loved you even then, but how could such an angel ever want me after so many years of berating and bullying?"

Heart full of love and grateful she'd never known about her inheritance, Gwen hugs him around the waist. "I've always loved you. That's why I hated you so much."

Through sobs, Honoria says, "I don't know how much more of this romance I can take."

Jane laughs and pats her back.

Unwrapping from the inappropriate hug, they join the group as Lord Everton brings in a bottle of champagne and insists that Robert toast with them.

"It's perfect, isn't it?" Gwen takes in the room full of people who care about her.

Theo stares into her eyes. "Yes. Perfect."

Thank you for reading A Lady's Christmas. I hope this book brought you into the holiday season. Weren't Gwen and Theo dreamy?

The good news is there are more Everton ladies to fall in love with. Start from the beginning with A Lady's Honor.

A LADY'S HONOR

Not every match is made at the marriage mart...

After a disastrous, short-lived engagement and years of caring for her ailing grandmother, Phoebe Hallsmith is resigned to spinsterhood. But if she must be unmarried, far better to be of use than languish at home, disappointing her parents. As an employee of the Everton Domestic Society of London, Phoebe accepts a position at the country home of an old friend and discovers an estate—and a lord of the manor—in a state of complete chaos.

. . .

L osing himself in the bottle has done nothing to ease Markus Flammel's grief over losing his wife. Not even his toddler daughter can bring him back from the brink. Now this fiery, strong-minded redhead has taken over his home, firing and hiring servants at will and arousing unexpected desire. As not one, but two suitors suddenly vie for Phoebe's hand, can Markus move past loss and fight for a future with the woman who has transformed his world?

CHAPTER 1

No. 6

Upon arrival, an Everton lady will seek the head of the
household and announce her presence and purpose.
—*The Everton Companion Rules of Conduct*

Y ears in Scotland caring for Grand had kept Phoebe from Rosefield and her best friend, Emma. Along the front of the grand estate, Emma's beloved rose bushes were overgrown and the facade loomed with sorrow and loss. Hesitating on the first step, she brushed aside her imaginings about the stones mourning Emma's death.

There were no words that could comfort Markus Flammel. What would she say?

A wayward branch from the rose bush lay in her path.

Rubbing the chill of October from her arms, she took a breath, clasped her bag with her Everton lady's companion inside and pulled her shoulders back. She had faced her grandmother's recovery and eventually her death; she could face this too.

She climbed the ten steps to the door and pushed aside her anxiety.

"This place is a bit unkempt, Phoebe." Honoria Chervil pranced up the steps beside her.

"Yes. That's part of why we are here, my lady." Phoebe grabbed the brass ring and knocked.

"We are arriving very early for paying a call. Perhaps we should have waited for the carriage to be repaired and come later with our belongings."

The hired hack rumbled back up the drive away from Rosefield. There would be no speedy escape.

Drawing a long breath, Phoebe pulled her shoulders back and her chin up. She was ready for whatever might come. "No. This is not a social call, Honoria. I did not wish to get a late start and it will take hours to have the wheel fixed at the inn. This will be better and the rest will follow this afternoon."

Glass shattered inside. Yelling and screaming and wood crashing sounded through the door.

"What on earth?" There was nothing worse than standing on the steps while screams and crashes filtered out. Phoebe pushed the door open.

As if her presence froze the scene, five pair of eyes stared at her in the threshold.

Two maids were on their knees surrounded by glass, faded flowers, and water. The round table lay in pieces behind them.

Mrs. Donnelly's bonnet was askew, her hair stuck out in all directions, and her chubby cheeks were as red as the overgrown roses in front of the house. The housekeeper scooped up a screaming toddler who was inches from getting into the dangerous glass.

Watson, the butler, stood like a statue staring at her with his hands in the air.

"What in the name of heaven is going on in here?" Phoebe never imagined her arrival would look anything like this.

Watson lowered his hands, smoothed his graying hair and approached. "I'm afraid you've caught us at an inopportune moment, my lady. The master has just arrived and we are preparing."

A maid sniffed as tears ran down her face and she used a rag to pull shards into a pile.

"Preparing for what?" Honoria asked.

"What on earth could be prepared by what I am witnessing?" Phoebe might have been out of line in questioning the staff of Rosefield before she'd even made her purpose known to Markus, but something was terribly wrong here.

Phoebe's mother had written about Emma's daughter, Elizabeth, being raised mostly by servants, but this was ridiculous. Elizabeth continued to wail as if being beaten with a stick and Mrs. Donnelly shushed her to no avail. Elizabeth grabbed a handful of Mrs. Donnelly's hair and they both shrieked until Phoebe's ears hurt.

"You might try back at another time, Miss Hallsmith." Sweat dripped down the side of Watson's long face.

Phoebe had a hundred questions, but would get no answers with the servants. What started as worry grew into annoyance, and she had to swallow down her emotions to remain calm. She turned to Mrs. Donnelly. "Madam, give me that child before she does you real harm."

Never had a woman of such girth moved with such speed.

She foisted Elizabeth into Phoebe's arms. "It's not Little Elizabeth's fault, Miss. She misses her father and he—"

"That will do, Mrs. Donnelly." Watson's scolding tone stopped any further explanation and started the maid crying again.

Phoebe propped Elizabeth on her hip. "You are far too small to be causing so much chaos. I cannot imagine what your sweet momma is thinking looking down on you. Now I expect you to act like a little lady."

Just like her father, Elizabeth had large green eyes, and they were wide open staring at Phoebe. A black smudge marred her left cheek and some kind of jelly stuck all around her rosy lips and pert little nose.

"She doesn't speak, my lady, though we try to teach her," Mrs. Donnelly said.

At two years old, Elizabeth should have some vocabulary. Phoebe's heart clenched. She should have come sooner. Of course, that hadn't been an option, but it did not soothe her guilt. "Well, we need no words for the moment. I'm sure when Miss Elizabeth has something important to say, she will do so. I do not go by a title any longer. Miss Hallsmith will do."

Elizabeth relaxed and her little body conformed to Phoebe's side as if they were two parts of a whole.

"You know, your mother and I were very good friends, Elizabeth. I think that you and I will be as well, but you must behave with more manners. Shall we go see your father?"

A wide smile showed off several teeth and brought a lovely pink to her sweet cheeks.

Watson stepped forward but kept enough distance as to not fall into Elizabeth's reach. "That's what started all of this, Miss. I'm afraid his lordship does not wish to see...anyone."

A low growl issued from deep in Elizabeth's chest.

Taking another step back, Watson paled.

"Ladies do not growl, Elizabeth. Where is his lordship?" Phoebe had spent years reining in her temper and learning to act like a lady even when she wanted to tear someone's hair out. It was becoming obvious that she would need to use all she had learned to get through the next few moments.

"In the study, but as I said, Miss Hallsmith, he does not wish to be disturbed." Watson held out his arms blocking her way.

Lifting Elizabeth higher on her hip, Phoebe turned toward the study. "I could not possibly care less about what his lordship wants. Lady Chervil, will you please wait here and explain our purpose?"

Honoria's chest puffed out as she lifted her shoulders and double chin. "I will be happy to, Miss Hallsmith."

Phoebe strode past Watson to the door and pushed through.

The enormous desk that Emma had purchased as a wedding gift for Markus took up most of the room. Phoebe's heart broke at the memory of how proud her friend had been of the custom-made gift. She had thought the sun rose with her husband, and the two had been the perfect couple. Wood, though dusty, paneled three walls while one boasted three large bookcases separated by two benches. A musty odor, from disuse and lack of cleaning, tickled Phoebe's nose.

Markus faced the cloudy window overlooking the side garden. "I do not wish to be disturbed. Go away."

The petulance of his tone only raised Phoebe's ire. Behavior of that sort should be disregarded, even if on the inside she seethed. Placing Elizabeth on the floor, Phoebe said, "That is too bad, my lord, as you have company who will not be turned aside. I am here on business."

His chair scraped across the wood floor as he stood and turned. He narrowed green eyes, shadowed with dark rings and sunken into pale skin, and he swayed. The strong, handsome man Emma had loved and married was no longer present in Markus Flammel.

Elizabeth froze.

Phoebe propped her fists on her hips and met his gaze.

"Phoebe Hallsmith?"

She dropped her hands and fell into a polite curtsy. "My lord."

"What are you doing here? Emma is gone."

His raised voice brought a whimper from poor Elizabeth who shrunk back and hid her face in Phoebe's skirt.

Turning, Phoebe called out the study door. "Mrs. Donnelly?"

Still frazzled and tattered, the housekeeper poked her head in the door. "Miss?"

"Please take Miss Elizabeth to the kitchen and see if Cook has a nice biscuit for her. Then see that her hands and face are washed before you bring her back here to visit with her father."

Mrs. Donnelly's face went white and she stiffened. "Little Elizabeth does not care for face washing."

"Do not tell me you are afraid of that child, Madam. I will not hear of it. Miss Elizabeth will be happy for the cookie and act the proper lady when it is time to wash. Isn't that right?" She gave Elizabeth a pointed look.

Red-faced, Elizabeth stared at Phoebe with her mouth open. Never taking her gaze away, she toddled over to Mrs. Donnelly and took her hand.

Once they left, Markus ran his fingers through his overlong hair. "How did you do that?"

Phoebe wanted to feel sympathy for him but she couldn't

keep her annoyance in check. "What on earth is wrong with you? How can you talk about Emma that way in front of your daughter? I am well aware of the loss of my dear friend, so your attempt to hurt me was wasted. Why is your house in chaos? Why are Emma's roses along the front entrance overgrown? Why is your staff terrified of a small child? Where have you been that they are shocked at your arrival? I demand answers."

"You demand? Who are you to demand anything? Where were you when Emma lay in her coffin and they covered her up with dirt? You have no rights here." He collapsed into his chair.

Guilt swelled inside Phoebe, and she sat across from him. "I was in Scotland with my grandmother. She was ill and I could not leave her. I received a letter from my mother about Emma's passing, and you may believe me when I tell you I was quite devastated. However, there was nothing I could do for her as she was and is in God's hands." Pulling herself together, she added, "I have been sent here by the Everton Domestic Society at the behest of your mother."

"I do not care why you are here. Get out of my house. You only serve as a reminder of her."

Where was the Markus of old? The man who Emma had gushed over. Markus would stop in and enjoy tea and conversation with the ladies. "Answer my questions. Then maybe I will leave you in peace."

He lifted a bottle of liquor out of his desk drawer, banged it onto the surface, removed the top, and took a long pull.

Phoebe had never seen this side of Markus. Running might have been the smart thing to do, but she held her place and swallowed her fear. He had always been calm and polite. Everything admirable had gone with her friend and the child suffered for it. Something had to be done. "Have you taken to the bottle as well as neglected your responsibilities, my lord? I always imagined you were smarter than your father."

Markus's face colored a horrible shade of purple, and he hurled the bottle across the room. It shattered against the wall in a starburst of glimmering shards. Brandy ran down the wall in rivulets and the stench of alcohol swamped the room.

If she left now, she could escape whatever wrath she had unleashed inside of him, but where would that leave poor Elizabeth? "Are you quite through or are there other objects you'd like to destroy? Maybe you will hack up that desk Emma bought you next?"

The air went out of him and he slumped onto his folded arms atop the desk. His shoulders rose and fell several times before he sat up. "I have not been home because everything here reminds me of her and I am not strong enough. As to your other questions..." He shrugged. "I fired the gardener and the child has put a strain on the household. Did you say my mother sent you?"

Many things she should have said, but his eyes shone from too much brandy and practical matters needed addressing first. "I work for Everton Domestic Society. Your mother contracted for someone to help you with Rosefield."

"Help me? How can you help me? No one can help." He put his forehead on his arms.

Nothing was ever easy. She needed a dozen questions answered, but one or two would have to do while he was in this state. "Why is there no nanny?"

"I may have fired one or two." He leaned his head back against the leather and closed his eyes.

"What about your mother? Has she not come to help with the staff?"

The green of his eyes was as intense as his daughter's. He scoffed. "I tossed her from the house the last time I was home. I think she said something about never darkening my door again. Just as well."

The situation was coming into view, and the remedy would not be an easy one. "I see. Lady Chervil and I each have a lady's maid. We will need rooms made up. I expect your staff can handle that small task. Our carriage needed repairs so we hired a hack this morning. The Everton Domestic Society's carriage with our bags and maids will arrive later today. They will need to be brought in. I will explain to your staff my needs and expectations."

He stood, and pressing his knuckles to the wood, leaned forward. If the desk had not been so big, his looming might have been threatening, but as it was, he was too far away to leave her awed.

"You cannot live here. I am an unmarried man," he said, voice cracking.

It wrenched her heart. "Everton's is aware of your situation. That is why Lady Chervil is here as my chaperon. She is speaking with Watson now."

Raising his voice, he pointed at Phoebe. "I do not want her or you here. I do not need you here."

"Your rage does not scare me, my lord, so you might as well save it for someone else. You could tell me you will hire a reputable nanny and allow her to sort out your house. You might tell me you have met a fine woman and plan to remarry. You could step up and be the man Emma married and take care of your own house. If you can look me in the eye and guarantee me these things will happen, I will walk out that door and report to my superiors that all is well here and leave you in peace."

He sank back into his chair. "I will not be responsible for you or Lady Chervil."

"No. I imagine you are not even responsible for yourself these days. One more thing, my lord. When Mrs. Donnelly arrives back here in a few moments with your daughter in tow, you are to put aside whatever sorrows you have and pay her the attention she deserves. Do I make myself clear?" If she was overstepping her boundaries, she didn't care. He had suffered, but so had Elizabeth and at his hand. There was no time like the present to start a change.

"She looks too much like Emma." Pain etched lines around his eyes and mouth.

Sympathy shared the space with her disgust. He was in pain but his behavior could not be ignored. "And quite a lot like you too, Markus. She is a smart child and she needs you."

Tugging at his badly tied cravat, he pulled it loose. "You have been here not twenty minutes. How do you know she's smart?"

Phoebe sat on the edge of the monstrous desk. "Your daughter is two years old and has not spoken, yet she clearly understands what is said to her."

He sat up. "Has not spoken?"

It took a force of will not to rail at him for being so self-absorbed he didn't know his child was mute. "According to your staff, Elizabeth does not speak. I think that is a sign of her intelligence."

"How so?"

"To be so filled with sorrow at her age that she chooses not to speak to anyone means she understands a great deal of what is happening in her world. Perhaps she has nothing to say in a world that left her without a mother and a father."

Staring down at his hands in his lap he nodded.

One scratch at the door and it opened. Elizabeth ran several steps into the room, stopped and stared at her father.

Softening his expression, Markus looked up. "Come here, Elizabeth."

Elizabeth looked from him to Phoebe. She spotted the broken glass on the far side of the room and took a step back.

Phoebe smiled. "It's all right. Go to your father."

Going to one knee, Markus opened his arms.

Blinking, Elizabeth cocked her head before running into his embrace.

It was all Phoebe could do to keep from breaking down into sobs at the sight of father and daughter hugging. What had she gotten herself into? She must be mad. If Emma had not been her closest friend, she would have left Markus Flammel and his problems to someone else at Everton. Though, now that she'd seen Elizabeth, she wanted to see her happy.

Mrs. Donnelly watched from the doorway. She dabbed her eyes with her apron and sniffed back her tears.

Lifting Elizabeth, Markus sat in his chair and propped her in his lap. "I am sorry I have not been at home, Elizabeth. I promise to try to do better."

Elizabeth put her palm on his cheek and father and daughter stared into each other's eyes.

It was a start. Phoebe shooed Mrs. Donnelly from the study, followed her, and closed the door, giving them some privacy. "I will need two rooms made up for Lady Chervil and myself. Once they are ready, I expect you to begin the process of getting this house cleaned. It is a crime how far Rosefield has fallen in two years. It is clear Elizabeth needs a proper nanny and Rosefield needs a gardener. I will put those things at the top of my list."

A wide smile spread across Mrs. Donnelly's face. "Will you be the new mistress here then, Miss Hallsmith?"

"Do not be ridiculous. I am an Everton lady. I shall help get his lordship back on his feet, if that is possible, and I will see that the house and child are in order. Once that is done, I will leave them to their life." Fear and sorrow spread through Phoebe's chest. Was she doing the right thing? Would Emma approve?

Her gut twisted as it always did when she imagined the end of an assignment. The client went on their happy way and Phoebe moved on to the next client's life. She never moved on with her own. Going to Scotland at the age of eighteen meant that she had missed several key seasons where she might have found someone to love. At twenty-four, Phoebe's time to find a husband and have a family was at an end. Everton's had been a boon for her. If not for Lady Jane, she would be listening to her mother and eldest brother natter on about how disappointing she was.

Phoebe sighed. "Watson, we arrived in a hired carriage as ours had a wheel that required fixing at the inn this morning. I expect it will arrive in a few hours with our maids and trucks."

Watson straightened his coat and smoothed his hair back. "I understand, Miss."

At least he was acting like a butler again. That was a small piece of progress. Phoebe would take some comfort in that. "Mrs. Donnelly, please knock on the study door in twenty minutes and take Elizabeth to the nursery. I am sure this will be very tiring for her."

"And for his lordship as well," Mrs. Donnelly said.

It was true, but Elizabeth was Phoebe's first worry. "I am less concerned with his lordship's condition. That child has suffered a lifetime. Well, her lifetime anyway."

"Miss, am I to understand that you will be taking over as housekeeper?"

Phoebe squeezed Mrs. Donnelly's hand. "I am not taking your position. I will leave when the house is in order. The viscount needs assistance and I need you to continue as the housekeeper Rosefield deserves. I would like to know: How have things gotten this bad, Mrs. Donnelly? Why have you not managed the house at least?" It was harsher than Phoebe had intended, but Rosefield was a mess. It was clear two years of neglect were at fault.

Mrs. Donnelly turned red and fussed with the keys at her waist. "I do not wish to speak against his lordship, Miss. He has been a good master for many years despite all the restrictions his father put on him. After my lady perished bringing the babe into the world, he was not the same man. More like the earl every day, he was. Drinking and disappearing for weeks on end. When he would come home, he'd fire half the staff. Some folks who had been in his service for years lost their posts for no good reason except his grief. It isn't possible to keep up a house of this size. We have only four of us left and the child to care for."

Horror smacked Phoebe in the face. "Four? You and Watson, the cook and one maid?"

"Cook was fired last year. The upstairs maid has been acting as cook. She's a fair one too."

"But it means there is only one maid for this entire estate." Drawing in a full breath, Phoebe made a mental list of all that would need her attention. "Things are far worse than I expected. It's a good thing I am here."

"Yes, Miss."

Honoria bustled in from down the hallway beside the stairs. "Do you know there is no staff in this house, Phoebe?"

Phoebe liked Honoria's directness, but sometimes wished she would save it for when they were alone. "I have just been informed, my lady. When the other carriage arrives, the driver and footman will have to bring our bags upstairs before they return to London. I will help get the rooms ready."

"Of course, my dear. I fear you have your work cut out for you." Sighing, Honoria ambled out the front door.

That much was certain. Wishing she had her grandmother's council, Phoebe climbed the stairs to find two guest rooms.

Emma's house was not the loving place it had once been,

and perhaps being estranged from her own family did not make Phoebe the perfect choice to correct things. Still, she was determined to create a safe place for little Elizabeth even if that meant removing the child. As she entered the first guest room, she prayed that would not be necessary. Emma would not want Markus to be left all alone. She shook off the dismal notion.

Also by A.S. Fenichel

HISTORICAL ROMANCE

The Wallflowers of West Lane Series

The Earl Not Taken

Misleading A Duke

Capturing the Earl

Not Even For A Duke

The Everton Domestic Society Series

A Lady's Honor

A Lady's Escape

A Lady's Virtue

A Lady's Doubt

A Lady's Past

A Lady's Christmas

The Forever Brides Series

Tainted Bride

Foolish Bride

Desperate Bride

Single Title Books

Wishing Game

Christmas Bliss

An Honorable Arrangement

HISTORICAL PARANORMAL ROMANCE

Witches of Windsor Series

Magic Touch

Magic Word

Pure Magic

The Demon Hunters Series

Ascension

Deception

Betrayal

Defiance

Vengeance

CONTEMPORARY PARANORMAL EROTIC ROMANCE

The Psychic Mates Series

Kane's Bounty

Joshua's Mistake

Training Rain

The End of Days Series

Mayan Afterglow

Mayan Craving

Mayan Inferno

End of Days Trilogy

CONTEMPORARY EROTIC ROMANCE

Single Title Books

Alaskan Exposure

Revving Up the Holidays

Visit A.S. Fenichel's website for a complete and
up-to-date list of her books.

www.asfenichel.com

WRITING AS ANDIE FENICHEL

Dad Bod Handyman (Lane Family)

Carnival Lane (Lane Family)

Lane to Fame (Lane Family)

Changing Lanes (Lane Family)

Heavy Petting (Lane Family)

Summer Lane (Lane Family)

Hero's Lane (Lane Family)

Icing It (Lane Family)

Mountain Lane (Lane Family)

Christmas Lane (Lane Family)

Texas Lane (Lane Family)

Building Lane (Lane Family)

Dragon of My Dreams

Turnabout is Fairy Play

Soul of a Vampire (Brothers of Scrim Hall)

Soul of a Reaper (Brothers of Scrim Hall)

Soul of a Dragon (Brothers of Scrim Hall)

Soul of a Wolf (Brothers of Scrim Hall)

Soul of a Demon (Brothers of Scrim Hall)

Soul of a Phoenix (Brothers of Scrim Hall)

Soul of a Monster (Brothers of Scrim Hall)

Mantus

The Manticore's Mate

Visit Andie's website for the most up to date list.

www.andiefenichel.com

About the Author

A.S. Fenichel (Andie Fenichel) gave up a successful IT career in New York City to follow her husband to Texas and pursue her lifelong dream of being a professional writer. She's never looked back.

Andie adores writing stories filled with love, passion, desire, magic and maybe a little mayhem tossed in for good measure. Books have always been her perfect escape and she still relishes diving into one and staying up all night to finish a good story.

Originally from New York, she grew up in New Jersey, and now lives in Missouri with her real-life hero, her wonderful husband. When not reading or writing she enjoys cooking, travel, history, and puttering in her garden. On the side, she is a master cat wrangler and her fur babies keep her very busy.

www.asfenichel.com

facebook.com/a.s.fenichel

x.com/asfenichel

instagram.com/asfenichel

bookbub.com/authors/a-s-fenichel

tiktok.com/@asfenichel?

pinterest.com/asfenichel

Made in United States
North Haven, CT
12 December 2023

45715227R10055